He reached out and gently traced his fingertip over the slant of her cheekbone. Her skin was as smooth as cream and he had no doubt it would taste just as rich.

His throat tightened as the urge to kiss her, make love to her began to tie his muscles into knots. "No. That's not what I want to do, Bella. But then you already know what you're doing to me. I imagine that makes you feel pretty damn good, doesn't it? Knowing you can make a big man like me weak in the knees."

Her eyes narrowed and then her head shook back and forth. "Why would you think such a thing? I have no desire to wield power over you. Or anyone else for that matter. That's one of the reasons I like being a lawyer. Because I believe everyone should be on equal ground."

"Well, in my case—"

"In your case, Noah, you're thinking too much. Worrying too much. Why can't you simply let yourself feel?"

"Because I'm feeling things that aren't good for me."

* * *

MEN OF THE WEST:
Whether ranchers or lawmen, these heartbreakers
can ride ~~about~~ **crazy...**

Dear Reader

A few books ago, when my Men of the West series migrated to Nevada, one of the first characters to appear was Noah Crawford. *Ahh!* For me, it was love at first sight. Even though he was in the background, I kept glancing his way and wondering what was going on behind his quiet, rugged face. It was plain he'd suffered some sort of tragedy and needed a special woman to help him heal. But when and where would he ever meet her? The man rarely stepped foot off the J Bar S.

Like me, Bella Sundell has had her eye on the reclusive ranch foreman for years, but he's always managed to keep a step ahead of her. Until fate steps in and Noah's running finally ends in her loving arms.

Noah's story is all about the healing power of forgiveness. I hope you'll join me on a ride down a desert canyon, where my hero finds a love of his own and a home he never expects.

May all the trails you ride be blessed with love and happiness.

Stella Bagwell

Her Rugged Rancher

Stella Bagwell

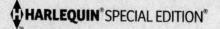

HARLEQUIN® SPECIAL EDITION®

Recycling programs
for this product may
not exist in your area

978-0-373-65958-6

Her Rugged Rancher

Copyright © 2016 by Stella Bagwell

This edition published by arrangement with Harlequin Books S.A.

For questions and comments about the quality of this book, please contact us at CustomerService@Harlequin.com.

Printed in U.S.A.

Having written over eighty titles for Harlequin, *USA TODAY* bestselling author **Stella Bagwell** writes about families, the West, strong, silent men of honor and the women who love them. She appreciates her loyal readers and hopes her stories have brightened their lives in some small way. A cowgirl through and through, she recently learned how to rope a steer. Her days begin and end helping her husband on their south Texas ranch. In between she works on her next tale of love. Contact her at stellabagwell@gmail.com.

Books by Stella Bagwell

Harlequin Special Edition

Men of the West

Christmas on the Silver Horn Ranch
Daddy Wore Spurs
The Lawman's Noelle
Wearing the Rancher's Ring
One Tall, Dusty Cowboy
A Daddy for Dillon
The Baby Truth
The Doctor's Calling
His Texas Baby
Christmas with the Mustang Man
His Medicine Woman
Daddy's Double Duty
His Texas Wildflower

The Fortunes of Texas: All Fortune's Children

Fortune's Perfect Valentine

Montana Mavericks: Striking It Rich

Paging Dr. Right

The Fortunes of Texas

The Heiress and the Sheriff

Visit the Author Profile page at
Harlequin.com for more titles.

To my editor, Gail Chasan, for letting me be me.
With much love and thanks!

Chapter One

Of all the damned luck!

Noah Crawford muttered the words under his breath as he rounded a curve of the narrow dirt road and spotted a slender young woman with long dark hair walking in the same direction he was traveling. A saddled bay mare followed close on her heels.

He jammed on the brakes and dust billowed as the truck and trailer came to a jarring halt. Up ahead, the woman quickly took herself and the horse off to the side, then with a hand shading her eyes, turned to see who'd made the untimely stop behind her.

Bella Sundell.

Her name shivered through him like an unwanted blast of cold wind. Hell's bells, what was she doing out riding in the middle of the afternoon? Why wasn't she in Carson City, practicing law with her brother?

He'd worked on this Nevada ranch for seven years

and during that time he'd never seen this woman on horseback. Nor had he spoken more than two dozen words to her. In fact, he often went out of his way to steer clear of her.

Too bad there wasn't some way to dodge her now, he thought, as he snatched up his gloves and climbed out of the truck. But she was his boss's sister. Besides, he wouldn't ignore anyone who needed help.

Striding across the hard packed dirt, he called out to her, "What's wrong?"

"Thanks for stopping, Noah." She pointed to the horse's front right foot. "She slipped on a rock and jerked a shoe loose when we were riding in the canyon. I thought I'd better lead her the rest of the way home. I didn't want to take the chance of damaging her hoof."

Trying to look anywhere other than her lovely, smiling face, he sidled up to the mare, then bent over to examine her foot.

"Riding in the canyon," he remarked. "That's a little risky for a woman alone, don't you think?"

Silence followed his question, but that hardly surprised Noah. She didn't have to answer to him. He was just the ranch foreman of the J Bar S, hardly her keeper.

Reaching into the front pocket of his jeans, he pulled out a Leatherman tool and quickly went to work jerking out the remaining nails of the loose shoe.

Behind him, he could hear Bella clearing her throat. "In case you hadn't noticed, it's the middle of May and the weather is already hot. It's shady and cooler down in the canyon. Especially along the creek bed."

"It might be cooler," he reasoned. "But it's rough terrain and a fair distance from home. Anything could happen to you."

"Anything could happen to me right here on the

road," she politely pointed out. "A cowboy not watching where he's driving could run over me and Mary Mae."

Like him? To argue the point with her would only end up making Noah look like a fool. A lawyer's job was to give advice, not take it. And this one was clearly no exception.

Turning his attention to the loose shoe, he levered off the piece of iron, then lowered the mare's foot back to the ground.

"Hang on, girl," he spoke softly to the horse. "We'll get you fixed."

After giving Mary Mae an affectionate pat on the shoulder, he forced himself to turn and look directly at Bella. The result was a familiar wham to his gut. The first time he'd met this woman, he'd been bowled over by her appearance. Creamy skin, long hair just shy of being black, warm brown eyes and soft expressive lips all came together to make one hell of a sexy woman. So much of a woman, in fact, that the passing years hadn't dimmed his reaction to her.

"When we get to your place I'll see about putting her shoe back on." He gestured to his truck and trailer. "Climb in. I'll get the mare loaded."

She hesitated and he realized she must have sensed his reluctance to become involved in her problem. Even though, to Noah, the loose shoe was a reasonably small problem. Bella was the big one.

"I'm sorry to put you out like this, Noah. If you're in the middle of doing something I can walk Mary Mae on home. It's not all that far."

"She doesn't need to keep walking on that bare foot. And I'm not in the middle of anything, except helping you," he said curtly.

Not waiting for her permission, he snatched up the

mare's reins and led the animal to the back of the long stock trailer. Once he had the mare loaded, he returned to the cab to find Bella already seated on the passenger side.

Climbing behind the wheel, he fastened his seat belt and started the engine. "Better buckle your seat belt."

She rolled her eyes at him. "Are you kidding? Here on the ranch?"

He slanted a glance in her direction, but the brief look was enough to take in her lush curves hidden beneath a pair of tight-fitting jeans and a white shirt left unbuttoned to a tempting spot between her breasts.

He let out a long breath. "That's right. Anything—"

"Can happen," she finished for him. "You've already said that. Is that your motto or something?"

Noah shoved the truck into gear. "If we had a wreck before we got to your place, you might be inclined to sue me for damages. With you being a lawyer and all," he added dryly.

The sound she made was something between a laugh and a groan. "Jett's a lawyer, too. Are you worried he might sue you if you ruin a piece of equipment or lose a calf?"

"No. Just making a point. It's better to be safe than sorry."

When Noah had first come to work on the J Bar S, Bella had been living up in Reno with her husband. But the marriage had fallen apart and Jett had convinced her to move in with him here on the ranch. She'd been working as a paralegal, but that job apparently hadn't been enough to suit her. In the past few years, she'd gone on to finish her education and pass the bar exam. Now she shared an office with her brother, Jett, in downtown

Carson City. He could say one thing for the woman, she certainly didn't lack ambition.

"Okay. To make you happy." Shrugging, she stretched the belt across her shoulder and locked it in place.

Noah let out a silent groan. He wouldn't be happy until he was finished with this woman and out of her sight. Just being this close to her bothered the hell right out of him.

"You're probably wondering what I'm doing out riding instead of practicing law," she said.

Was he that transparent? "It's none of my business."

She went on as though she hadn't heard his curt reply, "It's all Jett's doing. He urged me to take the day off and go shopping." She let out a dreary little laugh. "He thinks I've gone to Reno to buy dresses. I decided I'd rather go riding."

She probably had five or six closets stuffed with dresses and all the other fancy things a woman like her considered necessary. Noah figured she spent more money on one dress than his whole month's salary. But that was none of his business, either.

"I see."

She turned a curious glance on him. "Do you? I doubt it. Jett has this silly notion I'm sad because my old boss got married last weekend. He thinks I need to get out and get my mind off Curtis. Ridiculous. I'm not sad. And I never had my mind on Curtis in the first place. Not like that."

So what man do you have your mind on now, Bella?

The question was so heavy on Noah's tongue it was a struggle to bite it back. Hearing about her personal life was the last thing Noah needed or wanted. Of all the women he'd encountered since he'd left Arizona, she was the only one he'd ever given a second thought about. And though Jett sometimes casually mentioned his sister in conversation, Noah had never used the opportunity to ask his boss anything directly about Bella. No, Noah had learned the hard way that it was best to keep his distance from women and his thoughts to himself.

She said, "I suppose you never just ride for the fun of it. Your job forces you to spend a lot of time in the saddle."

His job was his fun, he thought. It was his whole life. With his eyes fixed on the narrow road, he asked, "Do you ride often?"

"Every chance I get. That's why I begged Jett to let me keep Mary Mae and Casper at my place instead of stalling them back at the ranch. Whenever I get the urge, I can saddle up and ride without having to drive back to the ranch yard."

Four years ago, Noah had been the only man working for Jett on the J Bar S. At that time his boss had owned only a small herd of cows, and a few using horses. But then Jett had met and married Sassy Calhoun and everything had changed. The couple had immediately started adding to the herd and purchasing adjoining land to support more livestock. In a matter of a few short months, the ranch had quickly grown to be too much for Noah and Jett to handle themselves. Especially with Jett still working as the Calhoun family lawyer and doing part-time private practice in town. Since then, five more ranch hands had been hired and Noah had been elevated to the position of ranch foreman.

"Yeah, Jett asked me about taking the two horses out of the working remuda. I told him we could manage without them."

From the corner of his eye, he could see her head turn

to look at him and the smile on her lips struck a spot so deep inside Noah, he hardly knew what had hit him.

"Hmm. When I first came to live with Jett, he only owned two horses. My, how things have changed," she said with wry fondness. "Now he has a whole string of horses, herds of cattle, and a wife and three kids."

When Bella had moved into the J Bar S ranch house with Jett, her brother had been single and trying to recuperate from a failed marriage of his own. The situation had worked well for the siblings until Jett had married Sassy and started a family. After the third baby arrived last year, Bella had decided her brother and his family needed their privacy. She'd had her own house built about a half mile from the main ranch house and almost within shouting distance of Noah's place. A fact that he tried to forget, but couldn't.

"Things around here have been growing all right," he finally replied.

The road grew steeper as it wound up the side of the mesa. Noah shifted the truck into its lowest gear and the motor growled as it climbed the switchback curves. Behind them, the trailer gently rocked as the mare braced her legs for the rocky ride.

When the vehicle finally crested the last rise, the land flattened and they entered a deep forest of ponderosa pine. After traveling a hundred yards under the thick canopy of evergreens, they reached the turn off to Bella's house.

A graveled drive circled in front of a two-story structure made of rough cedar and native rock, shaded by more pines. Since she lived alone, Noah had often wondered why she'd wanted so much space. To fill it with a bunch of kids, or was the huge structure just to impress her friends?

Pushing away both annoying questions, Noah parked the truck and trailer in a favorable spot to unload the mare, then killed the engine. "I'll fix Mary Mae's shoe and unsaddle her for you. Do you keep her stalled at the barn?"

She pushed aside the seat belt and reached for the door handle. "No. I have a little paddock fenced off for her and Casper. I'll show you."

He opened his mouth to assure her that he could handle the task alone, but before he could utter a word, she was already climbing out of the cab.

Cursing to himself, he left the truck and quickly strode to the back of the trailer. Bella was already there, shoving up the latch on the trailer gate.

Instinctively, he stepped next to her and brushed her hands aside. "That thing is heavy. Let me do it."

Thankfully, she moved back a few steps and allowed him to finish the task. But even that wasn't enough space to give Noah normal breathing room. Something about Bella made him forget who he was and why he'd turned his back on having a woman in his life. That was reason enough for him to get Mary Mae fixed as fast as he could and get the hell out of here before he started staring at her like a moonstruck teenager.

She stood watching, her hands resting on her hips. "Just because my job requires sitting at a desk doesn't mean I'm helpless and weak. I have muscles and I know how to use them, too."

"You can use them when I'm not around." He let the trailer gate swing open and immediately the mare backed up until she was standing safely on solid ground.

Bella immediately snatched a hold on Mary Mae's reins and Noah realized she had every intention of hanging around until this job was finished. So much for losing her company, he thought hopelessly.

"Do you have tools with you to deal with her shoe?" she asked.

"I have tools. Just not a big assortment of shoe sizes. This one I just took off still looks pretty straight. I can reset it," he told her.

"I didn't realize you were a blacksmith."

His gaze fixed safely on the mare, he said, "I'm not."

"What are you then, a farrier?"

"No. Just a guy who's taken care of horses for a long, long time. But if you'd feel better about waiting on a real farrier to fix Mary Mae, that's fine with me. He'll be coming by the ranch in a couple of weeks to deal with the remuda."

She didn't answer immediately and Noah glanced around to see she was looking at him with surprise. "Why would you think I'd want to wait?" she asked. "I don't want her going without a shoe for that long. Besides, I trust you."

She said the words so easily, as though she didn't have to think about them, as though she considered Noah worthy of handling any task she could throw his way. The idea caused a spot in the middle of his chest to go as soft as gooey chocolate.

"I'll get my things." He gestured to a flat piece of ground a few feet away. "If you'd like, you can take her over there in the shade of that pine."

Because he'd been helping the other ranch hands brand calves today, his shirt was still soaked with sweat while his caramel-colored chinks and blue jeans were marked with dirt and manure. No doubt he stunk to high heaven, but there was nothing he could do about sparing her the unpleasant odor. Except keep his distance. Something he'd do even if he smelled as fresh as a piece of sweet sage.

Beneath the cool shade of the pine, Bella stood near Mary Mae's head, keeping a steady hold on the reins, while her gaze remained fixed on Noah. With the mare's foot snug between his knees, he was bent over the up-turned hoof, carefully hammering nails into the iron shoe.

While he was totally absorbed with the task, Bella used the opportunity to study his big hands. The backs were browned by the sun and sprinkled with black hair. The fingers were long and strong. Just like him, she couldn't help thinking.

Six years ago when Bella had first come to live on the J Bar S, her brother had introduced her to Noah. At the time, he'd been the only man helping Jett take care of the sprawling ranch. In spite of her being numb from a fresh divorce, she'd found Noah's presence striking and unforgettable. But even then it had been obvious he wasn't a sociable man. He'd said little more than hello to her that day and since then she could count on one hand the times he'd spoken to her. Until today.

A few minutes ago, when he'd stopped along the road to check on her, she'd been totally surprised. Not that he was the type of man who'd ever say no to a woman in need of a helping hand. But this morning Jett had told her the men would be branding calves on the far side of the ranch today. She'd not expected to see Noah or any of the ranch hands on this section of the property.

The fact that Noah had been the one to happen by secretly pleased her. Of all the men Bella had encountered since her divorce, he'd been the only one who'd intrigued her. And to be totally honest with herself, he was the only one who'd turned her thoughts to the bedroom. She realized part of the reason for having such a sensual reaction to the man was his strong, sexy appearance. Yet he was also elusive, full of secrets and determined to keep his distance from her. Just the sort of man a woman liked to undress.

Funny, she thought, how Jett had believed she was besotted with Curtis, the lawyer she'd worked with for a few years before she'd passed the bar exam. True, she'd liked Curtis and admired his skills in the courtroom. And more than likely she would've gone on a date with him, if he'd ever felt inclined to ask. But he'd not asked and in the end, she'd been okay with that.

As for Noah, she'd never tried to catch his attention. He clearly didn't want to be her friend, or anything else. And she wasn't one to push herself on anyone. Besides, Jett had told her long ago that Noah was a very private man, who enjoyed the company of a horse far more than that of a human. There'd been many times she'd felt like that herself.

Pulling her thoughts back to the moment, Bella saw he was working quickly to snip off the excess ends of the nails he'd driven through the shoe and were now protruding through the outer wall of the mare's hoof. Using a big steel file, he smoothed away the residual bumps, then placed Mary Mae's foot back on the ground.

"All finished." He straightened to his full height and turned to face her. "The shoe should stay in place for a couple more weeks or so. By then she'll need four new ones anyway."

Bella nodded that she understood. "I'll make sure Jett sends the farrier up here to take care of her and Casper." She gestured toward the barn located several yards beyond the house. "I don't think you've seen my barn. After we get Mary Mae unsaddled I'll show you around."

As she waited for him to make some sort of reply, she lowered her lashes and slowly studied his face. For years a black beard had been a trademark of his appearance, but last spring Jett had commented about Noah shaving off his beard. A few days later, as she'd driven by the ranch yard, she happened to spot him from a distance. The change in his appearance had been dramatic, to say the least. And now that Bella could see him up close, she could admit she was mesmerized.

Noah was not a handsome man. Not by conventional standards, anyway. His craggy features were set in a wide, square-jawed face with a nose that was too big, and sun-browned skin that resembled the texture of a graveled road. Yet there was something about his dark blue eyes and strong quiet presence that oozed sexuality. And right now it was seeping out of his tough work clothes and going straight to her brain. But he clearly wasn't getting the same vibe from her. The taut look of discomfiture on his features said he wanted to excuse himself and run for the hills.

After a long stretch of awkward silence, he finally said, "Let's go."

With the mare following close behind her, Bella started toward the barn. The evening sun was beginning to wane and the air had cooled somewhat. The breeze whistling through the branches of the pines felt good against her face, but it couldn't do anything about the heat that Noah's presence was stirring up inside her.

Bella, you're a fool for having erotic thoughts about Noah Crawford. He's a loner. For all these years he's been content to live in a line-shack. He doesn't want a conventional life. And he especially isn't looking for a woman who wants a family of her own.

Disgusted at the nagging voice sounding off in her head, she mentally swatted it away and glanced over at the object of her thoughts.

"I imagine Jett told you that he tried to talk me out of building the barn."

"He mentioned it."

"Hmm. I'll bet he's done more than mention it," she said with a short laugh. "But as you can see, I don't always take my brother's advice. I wanted a place to keep my horses or whatever animals I might take a notion to get."

"What other kind of animals would you want?"

The doubtful tone of his voice didn't surprise her. People had all sorts of strange ideas about lawyers. He was probably thinking she considered herself above doing barnyard chores. Or maybe he thought the only things she knew about were depositions and plea deals.

"Oh, I think I'd like to have a few goats. I love the milk Sassy gets from her little herd. And I want to keep a few yearling colts around. Just for the fun of teaching them about being haltered and saddled—you know, basic training stuff."

"You know about dealing with yearlings?"

There was more disbelief in his voice and Bella refrained from shooting him an exasperated look. Except for what he probably heard through Jett, this man couldn't know much about her.

"Noah, I'm thirty-two years old. I know a little more than filing my nails and curling my hair. I've been around horses all my life. One of my best childhood friends lived on a horse ranch. We spent hours watching her father train and sometimes he allowed us to help. It was always fun. Now Sassy has the mustangs and I help her with them whenever my job allows me the free time."

She glanced over to see a stoic expression on his face. Which wasn't surprising. The few times Bella had been in his presence he'd not just kept his words to himself, he'd also hidden his emotions behind a set of stony features.

He said, "You might know the fundamentals, but exposing a yearling to a saddle and bridle is not for the faint of heart. It's dangerous."

"Dear Lord, Noah. The way you talk, simply living is a dangerous task."

"Maybe it is," he muttered.

She wondered what he meant by that, but knew better than to ask. Instead, she remained quiet and thoughtful as they walked the last few yards to the barn. Along the way, she listened to the jingle of his spurs and the faint flap of the leather chinks against his jeans. The sounds were those of a hardworking man and they comforted her in a way she'd never expected. She had no doubt that if he ever had a woman in his life, he'd certainly be able to take care of her, to protect her in all the ways a man could protect a woman.

When they reached the big red barn, Bella opened the double doors, then gestured for Noah to lead Mary Mae inside.

Once they were standing in the middle of a wide alleyway, Noah looked around him with interest. "You must've had the barn built of cinderblock for fire purposes."

"That's right. I'm sure that you know as well as I do that up here on the mesa, water is a scarce commodity.

And we probably live at least twenty miles from town and the nearest fire department," she reasoned.

"I didn't realize the barn was this big," he remarked. "From the road it looks smaller."

"Jett says I went overboard. But I wanted plenty of room." She pointed to a hitching rail made of cedar posts. Beyond it was a room with a closed door. "There's the tack room. Let's take Mary Mae to the hitching post to unsaddle her."

At the hitching rail, he gave the mare's reins a wrap around the post and proceeded to loosen the back girth on the saddle. While he worked, Bella decided to talk more about the barn. Hopefully, the subject would distract her from the sight of Noah and the way his broad shoulders flexed beneath the blue chambray shirt.

"Besides the tack room, there's six horse stalls and a feed room," she said, while thinking she sounded more like a real estate agent than a woman trying to make conversation with a sullen man. "The loft has plenty of space for several tons of hay, too."

"Very nice," he said.

Did he really think so? Or did he think she was just a girl with too much money to spend on things she knew nothing about?

The answers to those questions hardly mattered, she thought. She might have erotic fantasies about Noah, but he'd never be anything more than a ranch employee to her. After six years of ignoring her, he'd made it fairly clear he wasn't interested.

"Thanks. I'm proud of it."

It took only a few moments for him to finish unsaddling the mare. While he stored the tack and saddle away, Bella grabbed a lead rope and looped it around Mary Mae's neck.

"There's no need to put a halter on her. She'll lead like this," Bella explained. "Come along and after we put her out to pasture you can join me for coffee."

Even though she didn't glance his way, she could feel his eyes boring a hole in her back. As though she'd invited him into her bedroom instead of her kitchen.

"Uh, thanks, Ms. Sundell, but I'd better be getting on home."

Impatient now, she said, "My name isn't Ms. Sundell to you. It's Bella and furthermore, you know it. As for you getting home, you live not more than five minutes away. And there's still an hour or more before sundown. What's your hurry?"

Not waiting to see if he was going to follow, Bella headed down the alleyway until she reached the opposite end of the barn. There, she opened a smaller side door and urged the mare through it.

Once the three of them were outside, walking beneath the shade of the pines, he answered her question, "I have a busy day scheduled tomorrow. I need to rest."

A loud laugh burst out of her and from the corner of her eye, she could see the sound had put a tight grimace on his face.

"Rest? Right now I imagine you could wrestle a steer to the ground and not even lose your breath. You need to come up with a more believable excuse than that."

He moved forward so that he was on the right side of the mare's neck and a few steps away from Bella. "Okay," he said, "here's another reason for you. I'm nasty and sweaty. I don't need to be sitting on your furniture."

She laughed again. "It's all washable. Besides, I

made a rhubarb pie before I went riding. I'll give you a piece."

"I've never eaten rhubarb."

"Good. You're in for a treat."

"I don't think—"

She interrupted, "It would be impolite for you to refuse my invitation. Besides, the pie and coffee will be my payment for the shoe job. Fair enough?"

"I wasn't expecting payment."

No. He seemed like the type of man who didn't expect anything from anybody and it was that cool sort of acceptance that completely frustrated her.

Holding back a sigh, she said, "I realize that."

Bella hardly thought of herself as a femme fatale, but she figured most any single, red-blooded man would be happy to accept her invitation. For the pie, if no other reason. But Noah wasn't like most men. She expected if there was such a thing as a loner, he was the perfect example of one.

A short distance away from the east side of the barn, the pines opened up to create a small meadow. After she turned Mary Mae in the pasture to join Casper, she fastened the gate safely behind her.

"How do you water the horses?" he asked curiously.

"In spite of what I just said about water being scarce, I found a small spring with a small pool not far from here on a ledge of the canyon wall. The horses can access it easily and the pasture fence includes it. I try to check it daily to make sure it hasn't dried up."

"You're fortunate."

Bella knew he was talking about the water supply, but she couldn't help thinking that he was right in so many ways. After her divorce from Marcus, she'd not been able to see much of a future. Oh, she'd not given up on life by any means, but she'd certainly been bitter and disillusioned. Coming to the J Bar S, and living with her brother, had helped her get past the failure of her marriage. She might not have the family she always wanted, but at least she had a home of her own and a blossoming career as a lawyer.

"Believe me, Noah. I realize that every day." She turned toward the house. "Come on. Let's go have a piece of pie and you can tell me whether I can cook or not."

A few moments later, Noah followed Bella across a stone patio filled with lawn furniture and equipped with a fire pit. For entertaining her many friends, he thought. Most of them would probably be business people or folks connected to her law practice. He doubted a simple cowboy like him, who spent his days in the saddle, would be sitting under the shade of the pines, sipping summer cocktails.

They entered a screened-in back porch filled with more furniture and potted plants and then she opened a door that took them directly into a spacious kitchen equipped with stainless-steel appliances and a work island topped with marbled tile.

"Sorry for bringing you in the back way," she said. "But it would've have been silly to walk all the way around to the front door."

It was silly of him to be in the house in the first place, Noah thought grimly. In fact, he felt like a deer tiptoeing into an open meadow. He was just asking for trouble.

"I'm used to entering back doors, Ms.—uh, Bella."

She laughed softly. "Maybe one of these days you'll tell me about some of those back doors you've walked through."

Only if he was drunk or had been injected with sodium pentothal, Noah thought.

"That kind of confession might incriminate me," he said.

Her eyes sparkling, she laughed again and Noah felt the pit of his stomach make a silly little flip. Without even trying, she was the sexiest woman he'd ever met. And her sultry beauty was only a part of the reason. The richness of her voice, the sensual way her body moved, the pleasure of her laugh and glint in her brown eyes all came together to create a walking, talking bombshell.

"You need to remember that information shared between a lawyer and his client is private," she joked, then pointed to a long pine table positioned near a bay window. "Have a seat."

He looked at the table and then down at his hands. "I think I'd better wash my hands first."

Pink color swept over her face. "Oh, I'm sorry, Noah. I haven't really lost my manners. I just wasn't thinking. Follow me and I'll show you where you can wash up."

They left the kitchen through a wide opening, then turned down a hallway. When they reached the second door on their right, she paused and pushed it open to reveal an opulent bathroom.

"There's soap and towels and whatever else you need. Make yourself at home," she told him. "When you're finished you can find me in the kitchen."

"Thanks."

She left him and Noah entered the bathroom. At the gray marble sink, he scrubbed his hands and face with soap and hot water, then reluctantly reached for one of the thick, fluffy hand towels draped over a silver rack. If his hands weren't clean enough, they'd leave traces of dirt and manure on the towel. It would be embarrassing to have Bella discover he'd messed up her fine things.

Hell, Noah, why are you worrying about a damned towel or tracking up the tile? And why should you be feeling like a stallion suddenly led into a fancy sitting room instead of a barn stall? Bella isn't a snob. In fact, she acts as if she likes you. Why don't you take advantage of the fact?

Disgusted by the voice sounding off in his head, Noah hurried out of the bathroom. The sooner he accepted this payment of hers, the sooner he could get out of here and forget all about her and her warm smile and sweet-smelling skin. He could go back to being a saddle tramp. A man without a family and a past he desperately wanted to forget.

Chapter Two

When Noah returned to the kitchen, Bella was standing at the cabinet counter. The moment she heard his footsteps, she glanced over her shoulder and smiled at him.

"I waited about pouring the coffee. It dawned on me that since the day is so warm you might prefer iced tea."

He removed his gray cowboy hat and Bella watched one big hand swipe over the thick waves. His hair was the blue-black color of a crow's wing and just as shiny and she suddenly wondered if a thatch of it grew in the middle of his chest or around his navel. And how it might feel to open his shirt and look for herself.

"The coffee would be good," he told her.

Clearing her throat in an effort to clear her mind, she said, "Great. Well, if you'd like, you can hang your hat over there by the door and I'll bring everything over to the table."

He waited politely until she'd put the refreshments on the table and taken a seat, before he sank onto a bench on the opposite side of the table from her.

Bella cut a generous portion of the pie and served him, then cut a much smaller piece for herself.

"I'd offer to put a dip of ice cream on top, but I'm all out," she told him.

"This is more than fine," he assured her.

Even though he began to consume the pie and drink the coffee, Bella could see he was as taut as a fiddle string. Apparently he was wishing he was anywhere, except here with her. Strangely, the notion intrigued her far more than it bothered her.

From what Jett had told her, he'd often encouraged Noah to find himself a woman, but the man had never made the effort. If Jett knew the reason why his foreman shied away from dating, her brother had never shared it with her. And she'd not asked.

It would look more than obvious if she suddenly started asking Jett personal questions about his foreman. Still, she'd often wished an opportunity would come along for her to get to know more about the rough and rugged cowboy.

Now, out of sheer coincidence, he happened to be sitting across from her, without anyone around to listen in on their conversation. She wanted to make the most of every moment. She wanted to ask him a thousand questions about himself. And yet, she couldn't bring herself to voice even one. She didn't want to come across as a lawyer digging for information, any more than she wanted to appear like a woman on the prowl for a man.

"So how do you like your new house?" he asked.

Encouraged that he was bothering to make conversation, she smiled. "I do like the house. It's comfortable and meets my needs. But I have to be honest, there are times the quietness presses in on me. After living with Jett and Sassy and three young children, the solitude is something that will take time for me to get used to."

"I don't think Jett expected or wanted you to move out of his home."

She shrugged with wry acceptance. "I didn't want to end up being one of those old-maid aunts who got in the way and made a nuisance of herself."

She felt his blue gaze wandering over her face and Bella wondered how it would be if his fingers followed suit. The rough skin of his hands sliding along her skin would stir her senses, all right. Just thinking about it made goose bumps erupt along the backs of her arms.

He said, "I doubt that would've ever happened."

She grunted with amusement. "Which part do you doubt? Me being an old maid? Or getting in the way?"

"Both."

"You're being kind."

"I'm never kind," he said gruffly. "Just realistic."

Yes, she could see that much about him. A practical man, who worried about the dangers of life rather than embracing the joys.

"Well, it's all for the best that I moved up here on the mesa. Sassy and Jett need their privacy. I wouldn't be surprised if they had another child or even two to go with the three they have now."

"Wouldn't surprise me, either."

A stretch of silence followed and while she sipped her coffee, she watched him scrape the last bite of pie from the saucer.

When he put down his fork, she decided she'd better say something or he was going to jump to his feet and leave. And she didn't want him to do that just yet. Having him sitting here in her kitchen felt good. Too good to have it all end in less than fifteen minutes.

"Jett tells me the calf crop is turning out to be a big one this year," she commented.

"That's right. And Sassy has had some new foals born recently. Have you taken a look at them?"

"No. Unfortunately, I've been tied up with several demanding cases. But I plan to stop by the ranch house soon to see the kids. Maybe she'll drive me out to the west range to see them."

"You like being a lawyer?" he asked.

His question surprised her. She figured he wasn't really interested one way or the other about her personal life. But he'd taken the trouble to ask and that was enough to draw her to him even more.

"Yes, I do like it. That's not to say that I don't get exhausted and frustrated at times. But for the most part, I like helping people deal with their problems."

"Must be nice for you to get to work with your brother. Jett is easy to get along with. Me being here for seven years proves that," he added.

She smiled faintly. "Jett values your work, Noah. If it wasn't for you taking charge of everything I'm not sure he could even have this ranch. Aside from that, he cherishes your friendship."

"Yeah, well, I owe him a lot." Avoiding her gaze, he placed his cup on the table, then scooted the bench back far enough to allow him to rise to his feet. "The pie was delicious, Bella. Thanks. I can now say that I've eaten rhubarb."

Before she could stop herself, she blurted out, "Going already?"

He still didn't look at her. "I have chores at home to deal with."

"Then you probably don't have time for me to show you through the rest of the house?"

"Afraid not."

She tried to hide her disappointment when she spoke again, "We'll save that for next time."

He didn't reply to that and Bella figured he was probably telling himself there would be no next time. She'd never had a man make it so clear that he wanted nothing to do with her. But rather than put her off, it only made her more determined to spend time with him again.

As he gathered his hat from the rack on the wall and levered it onto his head, Bella stood and joined him at the door.

"I'll walk with you out to the truck," she told him.

"No need for that."

There wasn't any need, she thought. But she wasn't going to let him get away that easily. "Don't deny me. It's rare I have company of any kind."

They left the house the way they came in and as they walked toward his waiting truck, he said, "I imagine you have plenty of company, Bella."

She smiled faintly. "What makes you think that?"

"Jett does a lot of entertaining at home. And you two are brother and sister."

"Jett and I are siblings, but we think differently. Besides, most of his entertaining has to do with his law practice or ranching cronies. As for me, I don't normally mix business with my home. I have invited our mother over for a night or two, though. She thinks I need my head examined for building a house up here on the mesa, away from everyone. She'd go crazy from the solitude."

"And you haven't?"

That made her laugh. "Not yet. Of course, my sanity is subject to opinion," she joked.

He didn't smile. But then, she didn't expect him to. She'd never seen a genuine smile on his face.

By now they'd reached the driver's side of the truck. After he'd opened the door and climbed behind the wheel, he glanced at her briefly, then stared straight ahead at the windshield.

"You be careful when you ride in the canyon," he said.

She wanted to believe his warning was out of concern for her safety. Not because he was a bossy male. "I will. And thank you again for your help."

"No problem."

He closed the door and started the engine, leaving Bella with little choice but to step back and out of the way.

"Goodbye," she called to him. "And you don't have to be a stranger, you know. The sky won't fall in if you stop by once in a while and say hello."

He lifted a hand in acknowledgement, then put the truck into gear. Bella remained where she stood and watched the truck follow the circle drive until it disappeared into the dense pine forest.

So much for making an impression on the man, she thought. Noah hadn't even bothered to give her a proper goodbye. But then Noah Crawford wasn't like any man she'd ever met before. And that was darned well why she was determined to see him again.

Later that night, as Noah sat on the front step of his little cabin, he was still cursing his unfortunate luck of running across Bella. If he'd stayed with the men a half hour longer before heading home, he might have missed her. Or if she'd still been down in the canyon, he would've never known she was there or that her mare had thrown a shoe.

But for some reason, fate had aligned everything just right to put them on the road at the same time. No, fate had situated everything all wrong, he thought dismally. Now he was going to have a hell of a time getting Bella off his mind. After this evening, each time he passed her fancy house, he would think about too many things. How the kitchen had smelled of her baking, the way she'd talked and smiled as they'd sat at the pine table, and last, but hardly least, the way his heart had thudded like the beat of a war drum each time he'd looked at her.

Through the years Noah had worked for Jett, the man had never warned him to steer clear of his sister. Why would he bother? Both of them knew that Bella would never give Noah a serious look, anyway.

No, early on Noah had made his own decision to avoid Bella. Because he'd instinctively understood she was the sort of woman who could cause him plenty of trouble. Certainly not the devastating kind that Camilla had brought him, but enough to cause havoc in his life.

The sky won't fall in if you stop by once in a while and say hello.

Had she truly meant that as an invitation? he wondered. Or had she simply been mouthing a polite gesture?

What does it matter, Noah? Even if she meant it, you can't strike up a friendship with Bella. Getting cozy with her would be pointless. She's an educated lady, a lawyer with enough smarts to figure out a loser like you.

Shutting his mind to the mocking voice trailing through his head, he watched a small shadow creeping along the edge of the underbrush growing near the left wall of the cabin.

"Jack, if that's you, come out of there."

His order was countered with a loud meow and then a yellow tomcat sauntered out of the shadows and over to Noah. As the cat rubbed against the side of his leg, Noah stroked a hand over his back.

"Ashamed to show your face, aren't you? You've been gone three days. Hanging out somewhere with a girl cat, letting me believe a coyote had gotten you. I ought to disown you," he scolded the animal.

In truth, Noah was happy to have his buddy back. A few years ago, he'd found the yellow kitten all alone, on the side of the highway near the turnoff to the ranch. And though Noah had never owned a small pet before, he'd rescued the kitten and brought him home. Later on, when Jack had grown old enough to be considered an adult, the cat had made it clear to Noah that he was going to be an independent rascal. Whenever he got the urge, Jack would take off, then come home days later, expecting Noah to fuss over him as though nothing had happened.

"But I won't disown you," Noah said to the cat. "And you damned well know it."

Rising from the step, he opened the heavy wooden door leading into the cabin and allowed Jack to rush in ahead of him. Inside, Noah went over to a small set of pine cabinets and retrieved a bowl.

After filling it with canned food, he set it on the floor in a spot Jack considered his dining area. With the cat satisfied, he walked over and sank into a stuffed armchair. To the left of it, a small table held a lamp and a stack of books and magazines. Noah didn't own a television. Something that Jett often nagged him about. But

Noah had no desire to stare at a screen, watching things that would bore him silly. Instead, he'd rather use his small amount of time at home to read or listen to music.

Home. Most folks wouldn't call his cabin much of a home. Basically it was a two-room structure, with the back lean-to serving as a bedroom, while the larger front area functioned as a living room and kitchen. The log structure had been erected many years before, when Jett's maternal grandparents, the Whitfields, had owned the property. According to Jett, as the ranch had prospered, his grandfather, Melvin, had needed a line-shack and had built the cabin and its little native rock fireplace with his own hands. After a while, he'd upgraded the dirt floor to wooden planks and built on the extra room at the back. To Bella this cabin would be crude living, but to Noah, the simple space was all he needed. That and his privacy.

He was thumbing through a ranching magazine trying to get his mind on anything other than Bella, when his cell phone broke the silence. As he picked it up, he noted the caller was Jett.

"Did I wake you?" he asked Noah.

Noah rolled his eyes. "I'm not getting so old that I fall asleep in my chair before nine o'clock."

Jett chuckled. "I thought you might be tired after branding today. That's why I'm calling. Just checking to see how everything went."

Jett wasn't one of those bosses that called daily to line out the next day's work. Ever since Noah had taken this job, Jett had been content to let him run things his way and at his own pace. That was just one of the reasons Noah wouldn't want to be anywhere else.

"No problems," he told him. "One more small herd

to go—the one over on the western slope and we'll have them all branded. Can't do it tomorrow, though."

"Why not?"

"Used up all the vaccine we had. Me or one of the boys will have to go into town tomorrow for more."

"After I sent Bella home, I ended up being swamped with work today, but I would've found a way to go by the feed store and picked up the vaccine for you," Jett insisted.

"I thought about calling you. But we need a roll of barbed wire and a few more things anyway. Better to get it all at one time."

Besides working on selected days at his law office in town, Jett also acted as the lawyer for the Silver Horn Ranch, a position he'd held for years. Since his wife Sassy was a member of the Calhoun family, who owned and operated the notable ranch, Noah figured Jett would keep the job from now on.

"Well, there's no urgency about the branding. Whenever you and the boys can get to it will be soon enough. I don't plan to sell any of the calf crop on the western slope, anyway. I've given them to Sassy."

It wasn't surprising to hear Jett had given the calves to his wife. The man was always giving or doing something for her. On the other hand, Sassy deserved her husband's generosity. She'd given him three beautiful children, worked hard to make the ranch a success, and most of all she adored him. Jett was a lucky man and he knew it.

"I—uh, ran across your sister today," Noah said as casually as he could. "She'd gone riding and her mare had thrown a shoe."

"Yes. I spoke with her earlier over the phone. She was very grateful for your help. Thanks for lending her a hand, Noah. You know, she's very independent. I'm surprised she didn't tell you she'd take care of the mare's shoe herself."

Noah rose from the chair and walked over to the open door. If he looked to the southwest, he could see the lights from Bella's house, twinkling faintly through the stand of pines. Now that he'd been inside her home, it was much too easy to picture her there.

"She didn't put up a fuss," he replied.

Had Bella told her brother that she'd invited him inside for pie and coffee? Noah wondered. The memory of his brief visit with her still had the power to redden his face. Looking back on it, Bella had probably thought he was a big lug without enough sense to paste two sentences together. Even now in the quiet of his cabin, he couldn't remember half of what he'd said to her.

"Speaking of fussy, I wish you'd stop being so damn hard to please and try to find yourself a woman," Jett said.

"That isn't going to happen," Noah muttered. "Not ever."

"Never say never, Noah. You don't know what the future holds for you."

"My future damned sure won't have a wife in it!"

His outburst was met with a moment of silence, then Jett said, "Well, I'm glad to hear you're feeling like your old self tonight."

Noah swiped a hand over his face. When he'd first responded to Jett's ad for a ranch hand, he'd expected him to ply him with all sorts of questions. That was the nature of a lawyer, he figured. But the only facts Jett had seemed interested in was whether Noah had experience taking care of cattle and if he was wanted by the law. It wasn't until time had passed and a friendship had developed between the two men that Noah had confided he'd left a bad situation behind him and it had involved a woman. Jett had seemed to understand it was a matter that Noah wanted to keep to himself and he'd never asked him to elaborate. Still, that didn't stop his friend from urging him to find a wife.

A wife. The idea was laughable.

"Why wouldn't I be feeling like my old self?" Noah asked grumpily.

Jett said, "Oh, I don't know. One of these days you might soften up and be a nice guy for a change. Miracles do happen."

Before Noah could think of a retort, Jett went on, "I got to go help Sassy. She's trying to get the kids to bed. If you need me tomorrow, call me."

"Yeah. Good night, Jett."

Ending the conversation, Noah slipped the phone into the pocket of his shirt and stepped back outside. The night air had cooled and the clear sky was decorated with endless stars. A gentle breeze stirred the juniper growing at the corner of the cabin and somewhere in the canyon he could hear a pack of coyotes howling.

Normally he savored soft summer evenings like this. But tonight he was restless. Being near Bella has stirred up dreams and plans that he'd pushed aside long ago.

This job was all that he wanted and his friendship with Jett was too important to let a woman ruin it, he thought grimly.

I wish you'd...try to find yourself a woman.

Noah's jaw tightened as Jett's remark echoed through his mind. Even if he wanted a wife, it would be impossible for him to find one. Ever since he'd first laid eyes on Bella, he'd not been able to see any other woman but her.

Feeling something move against his leg, he looked

down to see Jack sitting on his haunches, peering up at him.

"Yeah, Jack, I know I'm a fool of the worst kind. But you're not in a position to be pointing fingers. You do enough womanizing for the both of us."

The remainder of the week was a busy one for Bella. Between two heated divorce cases, an adoption case, plus a custody trial, she'd hardly had time to eat or sleep. And it didn't help matters that Noah had continued to pop into her mind at her busiest moments, playing havoc with her ability to focus on her work.

Ever since he'd stopped on Tuesday afternoon to help her with Mary Mae, she'd not been able to push the man out of her mind. Now it was Sunday afternoon and as she sat on the back porch listening to the lonesome sound of the wind whistling through the pines, she could only wonder if he was at his cabin and what he might think if she showed up on his doorstep.

You're thinking about him because he's a mystery, Bella. Because he's lived alone in that line-shack for all this time and you don't understand why he's such a recluse. That's the only reason the man is dwelling in your thoughts. That's the only reason you want to see him. Just to satisfy your curiosity.

The mocking voice in her head caused her to sigh with frustration. Maybe Noah's solitary life did intrigue her, yet there was much more about him that played on her senses. If she'd been more like some of her daring girlfriends, she would've already made an effort to try to catch his attention. But she wasn't the type to pursue a man. Besides, how did a woman go about garnering the attention of a man as cool and distant as Noah? If she knew the answer to that she might have tried years ago.

The other day when he'd helped her with Mary Mae, she'd caught quick glimpses of what was hidden behind his blue eyes and rugged face. And those few peeks had been stuck in her mind, tempting her to see him again.

Tired of fighting a mental battle with herself, Bella rose to her feet and hurried into the house. Mr. Noah Crawford might as well get ready for company, she decided, as she stepped out of her skirt and into a pair of riding jeans. Because he was about to have a visitor, whether he wanted it or not.

Less than a half hour later, Bella reined Casper, her gray gelding, to a stop beneath the shade of a tall cottonwood and slipped from the saddle. After she'd secured the get-down rope to a strong limb, she approached the cabin.

Although there were no sounds coming from the log structure, the door was standing wide open, as were the two windows facing the front yard. Not that the space could actually be called a yard, she thought. It was mostly a thick carpet of pine needles with patches of bramble bush and Indian rice growing here and there.

At the doorstep, she shoved her cowboy hat off her head. A stampede string caught at the base of her throat, allowing the headgear to dangle against her back. After running a hand through her hair, she rapped her knuckles against the doorjamb.

"I'm here."

Jerking her head in the direction of his voice, she spotted Noah standing a few feet away at the corner of the cabin. One look at his tall, dark image was enough to push her heartbeat to a fast, erratic thump.

Unconsciously, her hand rested against the uncomfortable flutter in her chest. "Oh, hello, Noah! I didn't see you when I knocked," she said.

"I was at the back of the house," he explained. "I heard you ride up."

Heard her? Casper hadn't neighed or even kicked over a small stone. He must have superhuman hearing, she decided.

"I was out riding and thought I'd stop by to say hello." The explanation for showing up on his doorstep sounded lame, but it was the best she could do. She could hardly tell him she'd purposely invited herself.

His sober expression said he didn't believe a word she'd just said. Yet she found herself smiling at him anyway. Mostly because something about him made her feel good inside.

He said, "At least you're not riding down in the canyon."

She smiled again. "No. But that doesn't mean I've marked that riding trail off my list. It's too beautiful to resist."

He looked different today, Bella realized, as her gaze took in his faded jeans and gray T-shirt. The few times she'd been in Noah's presence, he'd always been dressed for work with long-sleeved shirts, spurs strapped to his high-heeled boots, and a gray felt on his head. She'd never seen his bare arms before and the sight had her practically gawking. She'd not expected them to be so thick and muscled, or his skin to be nut-brown.

"So you're riding the gelding today," he remarked. "Is the mare okay? Any problem with her foot?"

"No problem. I just thought it was Casper's turn to get out for a while."

He didn't say anything to that and Bella figured he was waiting for her to say she needed to mount up and finish her ride. Well, that was too bad. She wasn't going to let him off that easily.

"Uh, am I interrupting anything?" she asked politely.

He hesitated, then said, "I was just putting some meat on the grill. On Sunday I usually make myself an early supper."

"Mmm. I don't suppose you'd have enough for two, would you?"

His brows shot up, but Bella was determined not to feel embarrassed by her forward behavior. It wasn't as if she was asking him to kiss her.

"It's only hamburgers," he said.

"I love burgers. Especially when they're grilled. Are you a good cook?"

"I can't answer that. I'm the only one who ever eats my cooking."

She chuckled. "Then you really need for me to give it a try. I'll give you an honest review."

His attention lifted away from her to settle on Casper. Bella was glad to see the horse already understood he'd reached his destination. His head was bowed in a sleepy doze, his hind foot cocked in a relaxed stance.

Noah said, "Bella, I think—"

Bella quickly interrupted, "If you don't have enough food to share, that's fine. A cup of coffee will do me."

He grimaced. "It's not the food. I—"

"Don't like my company?" she asked pointedly.

Dark color swept up his neck while the frown on his face deepened. And watching his reaction, Bella could only wonder if she'd gone crazy. The man clearly didn't want her around. Any sensible woman would proudly lift her chin and walk away. But there was something in his eyes that made her stand her ground. A bleak, desperate look that called to her heart.

He blew out a long breath. "I wasn't expecting you, that's all."

She stepped off the porch and walked over to him. "I apologize for showing up unannounced. But it's a lovely afternoon and I was getting very tired of my own company."

Then why didn't she drive down to her brother's house, where she could find plenty of company? Noah wanted to ask. Why didn't she get on her horse, ride off and leave him alone?

If Noah was smart, he'd do more than ask her those questions. He'd tell her outright that he didn't want her around here messing with his mind, making him feel things he didn't want to feel. But he couldn't bring himself to utter any of those things to her.

Just seeing her again was making his heart thump with foolish pleasure. Hearing her sweet voice was like the trickle of a cool stream to a man lost in the desert. He couldn't forbid himself those pleasures. Even if they might eventually hurt him.

"Well, it just so happens I have enough food to share." He gestured toward the open door. "If you'd like to go in, I'll see about making another patty for the grill."

"Thanks. I would like."

Noah followed her inside the cabin and moved to one side as she stopped in the middle of the room to glance curiously around her. He could only wonder what she thought about the log walls, low-beamed ceiling and planked floor, much less the simple furnishings. But then, he'd not invited her up here for a visit, he thought. She'd invited herself.

"This is cozy. And so much cooler than outside," she commented, then glanced at the short row of cabinets built into the east wall of the room. "Those are nice. Did you help build them?"

Did she actually believe he might be that talented? The idea very nearly made him smile, but he stopped himself short. What the hell was he doing? He didn't smile at women. He didn't even like them. Not after the hell Camilla had put him through.

"I helped measure and hammer a few nails, but not much more than that. When it comes to carpenter work I can do a few repair jobs, but nothing major."

She said, "I made a little doghouse once with the help of my grandfather. It turned out pretty good, but the darned dog never would get in it. Probably because Grandmother kept letting him in the house."

The main ranch yard of the J Bar S sat just across from Jett's house. While Bella had lived there, Noah had often spotted her going to her car as she left for work in the mornings. And sometimes late in the evening as he'd dealt with barn chores, he'd seen her return. She would always be wearing dresses and high heels and carrying a leather briefcase. With that image fixed in his mind, it was hard enough to accept she was a competent horsewoman, much less imagine her using a hammer and nails.

"Sounds like your grandmother spoiled your project," he said.

"Not really. My cats used it."

He inclined his head in the direction of the windows. "I don't get much sunlight in here. I'll turn on a lamp."

"Don't bother on my account. I can see fine."

Noah wasn't having any trouble seeing, either. Yet he was having a problem deciding if the vision standing in his cabin was real or imagined. Other than Jett and a couple of the other ranch hands, he'd never had visitors up here. And bringing a woman home was definitely off-limits. How Bella had managed to be here was a different matter. But she was here just the same and for now he'd try to deal with the situation as best he could without being rude.

"Have a seat. The couch is a little hard. You might find the chair more comfortable."

"Thanks, but I'll sit later. Let me help you with the hamburger meat. I can make the patty."

She followed him over to the kitchen area and though she stood a few steps away from him, Noah felt completely smothered by her presence.

"I'll do it," he told her. "You're a guest."

Laughing softly, she leaned her hip against the cabinet counter. Noah tried not to notice how her jeans hugged the ample curve of her hips and thighs and the way her blouse draped the thrust of her breasts. And even when he looked away, the image was still so strong in his mind it practically choked him.

"I'm not a guest," she reasoned. "I'm just a neighbor who's intruded on your privacy. But thanks for letting me."

Why did she have to be so nice? Why couldn't she be one of those spoiled, abrasive women that got on everyone's nerves? Why couldn't she be a woman who considered herself too good to come near his cabin, much less enter it? Then he wouldn't be having this problem. He wouldn't be wanting to throw caution to the wind and let himself simply enjoy her company. Instead, she was warm and sweet. And just having her near filled him with a hollow ache.

"Well, I don't normally have company. Uninvited or otherwise," he told her. "So my manners are a little rusty. I'm afraid you'll have to overlook them."

He glanced her way to see she was smiling and for a moment his gaze focused on her dark pink lips and white teeth. That mouth would taste as good as her voice sounded, he imagined.

"Who's worried about manners? You and I are family," she said. "Well, practically. You've been here on the ranch longer than I have. We just never had the opportunity to talk much. When I was still living with Jett, you would stop by, but never say a word to me. I'm glad you're being much nicer today."

He laid a portion of ground meat onto a piece of wax paper and smashed it flat. "A guy like me doesn't have anything interesting to say to a lady like you."

From the corner of his eye he watched her move a step closer. "Lady? I've not had a man call me that in a long time, Noah. Thank you."

Her voice had taken on a husky note and the sound slipped over him like a warm blanket in the middle of a cold night.

"That's hard to believe, Bella."

She shrugged. "Not really. Men aren't very chivalrous nowadays. At least, not the ones I cross paths with. Maybe that's because of my profession. In the courtroom they see me as an adversary. Not a lady."

"Jett says you worked hard to get your degree. He also says you're good at your job."

"Jett is obviously biased. But I can credit him for getting me in the law profession. When I was growing up, I never dreamed of being a lawyer. But after Marcus and I divorced the course of my life changed. Jett got me interested in being a paralegal and from there I guess you could say I caught the bug to be in the courtroom."

Her gaze fell awkwardly to the floor and it suddenly dawned on Noah that every aspect of this woman's life hadn't been filled with success. She'd endured her own troubles with the opposite sex. And though he'd heard Jett label his ex-brother-in-law as a liar and a cheat, Noah had never questioned the man about Bella's divorce or how it had affected her. It was none of his business. But that didn't stop him from wondering how much she'd really loved the guy.

Or whether she was finally over him.

Chapter Three

Clearing his throat, Noah said, "Excuse me, Bella, but I'd better take this out to the grill. It's probably hot enough to put the burgers on now."

"Sounds good," she told him. "I'll join you."

She followed him out of the cabin and around to the back. Although there were only a few clumps of grass growing here and there over the sloping ground, he kept it neatly mown. For a makeshift patio, he'd put together four flat rocks. On one corner of the space, he'd erected a small charcoal grill atop a folding table.

A few steps away sat a lawn chair made of bent willow limbs and cushioned with a folded horse blanket. Near it lay a huge pine trunk that had fallen long before Noah had ever moved into the cabin. The smooth, weathered log made a playground for squirrels and chipmunks and a seat where he often drank his morning coffee.

While he positioned the patties on the hot grill, Bella ambled a few feet away where the forest opened up to a view of bald desert mountains in the distance.

"Are those mountains on Jett's land?" she asked.

It surprised Noah to hear her call it Jett's land. He'd always suspected that she was a partial owner in the ranch, but apparently he'd supposed wrong.

"No. They look close, but they're at least ten miles away. Why do you ask?"

"Just curious. This is going to sound silly, but there are places on this ranch that I've never seen. Especially since Jett and Sassy bought the adjoining land a few years ago."

"You obviously knew your way to the cabin," he said.

"That's right. My grandparents built the cabin," she told him. "And when I was a little girl, my grandmother and I would come up here in the summer and pick wild berries."

"I met your grandparents back before Christmas, when they came up to see little Mason after he was born. Nice folks."

"Yes. I keep promising to drive down for a little visit with them, but it seems like I can never get that many free days in a row to make the trip to California." She turned and strode back to the shaded area where he was standing. "One of these days I'm going to clear my work schedule and go anyway. My grandparents aren't getting any younger and I want to enjoy them while they're still around."

"Melvin talked to me about the little ranch he owns now. I'm glad he's still healthy enough to have horses and cattle."

Ignoring the chair, she sank onto the pine truck and crossed her ankles out in front of her. Noah closed the lid on the cooker and took a seat in the lawn chair a few feet away from her.

"Do you have grandparents, Noah?"

He said, "The only grandparents I ever really knew have passed on. Mom's parents were never around, so I have no idea if either of them are still alive or where they might live." The look of surprise in her eyes prompted him to add, "I don't know where she or my dad are, either. They divorced when I was thirteen. After that, Mom left and never came back. Dad stuck around for a few months, then left me to be raised by his parents."

Just as he'd expected, she looked stunned. And that was exactly why he'd revealed that part of his upbringing to her. He wanted to make sure she understood the sort of background he'd come from. That he'd been a child his own parents hadn't wanted and his grandfather had merely tolerated.

"Oh. I didn't know. Jett never mentioned the circumstances of your parents to me."

"That's because I've never talked to Jett about them. Your brother and I mostly talk about the present and the future."

"Yes. Well, Jett has some pretty awful memories of his own that he'd rather leave in the past. Most of us do."

She smiled at him and Noah was surprised to see she was still looking at him as though she liked him, as though he was someone she wanted to spend time with. He could only think she was either a very bad judge of character, or a very special woman.

The scent of the cooking beef began to fill the air and Noah got up to check on the progress of the burgers.

While he flipped the meat, she asked, "Do you like living here in the cabin? Away from everyone?"

"I'm a simple guy, Bella. I have everything I need or want right here." At least that was what he'd been telling himself since he'd arrived in Nevada. But there were plenty of days Noah still felt the nagging need for a place of his own, and even more nights when he imagined himself with a wife and children to nurture and love. Yet once he'd left Arizona, he'd vowed to live a solitary life and so far, he'd had no trouble sticking to that sensible choice. Whenever he got to feeling like Jack, and the urge to go on the prowl for a woman hit him, all he had to do was think about Camilla. Remembering all the lies she'd told doused his urges even better than a cold shower.

"I guess the cabin seems pretty crude to you," he added.

"I wasn't thinking about the cabin," she told him. "I was wondering if you ever get lonely."

For most of his thirty-five years, Noah had been lonely. As a kid, he'd had buddies in school, but he'd never been able to invite them to his house for a meal or a simple game of catch in the backyard. Not that he would've been embarrassed by the Crawfords' modest home situated on the poor side of the tracks. Most of his friends had been just as impoverished as the Crawford family. No, it had been his parents' violent arguments that had ruined his chance to be a normal kid. And later, well, he'd let himself trust in another human being and ended up learning he couldn't depend on anyone to stick by him. Not even a good friend.

"I don't have time to get lonely," he lied. "Every morning I leave here before daylight and usually don't return until dark. That doesn't leave me much time to pine for company."

It wasn't until he'd put the lid back on the grill and

risen to his feet that she said, "It must be nice to be that contented with your own company. I'll be the first to admit I get lonely."

He grimaced. "You should have stayed in your brother's house. With all those kids there's never a dull moment."

She shrugged. "I was getting in the way."

"Jett didn't want you to move out. I don't suspect Sassy did, either."

"Both are too nice to admit they were sick of Aunt Bella being underfoot—" she smiled wanly "—but I figure you probably understand how it feels to be, how should I say, standing on the outside looking in."

Noah had to choke back a mocking groan. She, or anyone else, couldn't possibly know how he'd felt as a child. His parents had barely acknowledged his existence. They'd been too busy trying to tear each other down. And later, his grandfather had only been interested in getting him raised to an age where he could kick him out into the world. Yeah, Noah knew all about being on the outside. But Bella didn't need to know everything about his broken childhood, or the years that had followed before he'd finally settled here on the J Bar S. She'd probably feel sorry for him, and he didn't want that from her, or anyone else.

He sank back into the lawn chair. "I understand, Bella. More than you think."

She sighed. "While I was married and living in Reno I never imagined I'd ever be calling the J Bar S my home. I expected to stay in the city and raise a family with Marcus. Now I've been here nearly six years and Jett is the one with the family. I'm not a mother, but at least I'm a lawyer," she added wryly. "Guess I should be thankful all these years haven't been totally wasted."

So in spite of her ex-husband deceiving and hurting her, she still she wanted a husband and family. He couldn't decide whether she was a glutton for punishment, or a very brave woman.

"Looks to me like you've had a pretty successful life so far," he replied. "A person has to learn to appreciate the blessings they have, instead of always wanting more."

From the corner of his eye he could see her frowning. The expression was much easier to deal with than her smiles. As long as she disapproved of him, the less likely he'd be to lose his senses around her.

"Hmm. You're saying I should be satisfied with what I have?"

He turned his head to look at her. "Well, you have a lot more than most, Bella."

She gazed thoughtfully toward the mountains in the distance. "Yes, probably so. But a woman likes to dream, Noah."

Oh yes, he thought bitterly. Noah knew, firsthand, how a woman could fantasize. Unfortunately, in Camilla's case, her dreams had been twisted and wrapped solely around him. It hadn't mattered to her that Noah and her husband, Ward, had been the best of friends and partners in Verde Canyon Ranch. No, she'd tried to make her dreams come true, no matter the consequences. As a result all three of them had been thrown into a nightmare, one that Noah still couldn't forget.

Giving himself a hard mental shake, he got to his feet. "I'd better check the meat," he told her.

Five minutes later, Noah was carrying a platter of sizzling patties into the cabin with Bella following close behind.

"Too bad you don't have a picnic table of some sort," she remarked. "It would be nice to eat outside."

"If you'd rather eat outside, we can. But it's a nuisance trying to balance everything on your lap."

Bella shook her head. "This is fine. It's just that the weather is almost perfect and I love eating outdoors. We'll do it some other time—at my house."

He didn't say anything to that and Bella figured hell would probably freeze over before she ever got him to visit her house again. But she wasn't going to think about that now. At least she was getting to spend time with the man and he was talking much more than she'd ever expected him to.

He placed the platter of meat on a small round table positioned beneath one of the open windows, then added a tray of prepared vegetables he'd taken from the refrigerator.

"I don't have any tea or soda," he told her, "but I can offer you a beer or water."

"Beer goes perfect with a burger," she told him. "Is there anything I can do to help? If you'll show me where you keep your dishes and silverware I'll set the table."

He slanted a look at her as though he wasn't sure he wanted her to be milling about in his kitchen, but after a moment he motioned his head toward the cabinets.

"The plates are in the cabinet on the left. The silverware is in the drawer underneath."

While she set the tiny table, he fetched the drinks and a bag of potato chips. Once everything was ready, he surprised her by pulling out one of the scarred wooden chairs and helping her into it.

His nearness stirred her like nothing she could remember and though she told herself she was being foolish, she couldn't seem to slow the erratic beat of her heart or stop the excitement rushing through her.

"Thank you, Noah."

He took his seat across from her and as they began to put their burgers together, Bella asked, "Are you finished with all the branding now?"

"We wound it up yesterday. Now it's time to deal with a bunch of fencing. The men won't like it but that's okay. They can't have fun every day."

Bella smiled as she added salt and pepper to her burger, then pressed everything inside a bun covered with sesame seeds. "Does that mean they consider branding as fun?"

"The lucky ones who get to rope and drag calves to the fire think of it that way. The hands working on the ground might have different ideas. They have the hardest job. That's why after a few hours I make the men change places."

It wasn't surprising to hear Noah tried to keep things fair. As the foreman over a group of ranch hands, she expected he was always evenhanded. But how would he be as a lover or husband? Would he see her as his equal? Or was he an old-fashioned man who would expect his woman to submit to his wants and wishes?

Oh, Lord, Bella, why would you be wondering about those sorts of things? It's clear he doesn't want a family. You need to snap out of these silly daydreams you're having about this cowboy. One of these days you'll cross paths with a guy who's meant to be your soul mate. And it's not elusive Noah.

Shutting her ears to the voice going off in her head, she bit into the hamburger and immediately groaned with pleasure.

"Mmm. You're a good cook, Noah. This is delicious."

He shrugged. "I've cooked my own meals ever since I was a kid. So I've had plenty of practice."

Had he fixed his own meals out of necessity, she wondered. Or simply because he'd wanted to? From what he'd said, his parents had more or less abandoned him. But surely his grandparents had been around to see to his needs. Or had they? She wanted to ask him, but reminded herself that Noah wasn't on the witness stand or even sitting across from her desk at the office.

Eventually, she decided to ask something a little less personal. "Did you grow up here in Nevada?"

For a moment she thought he wasn't going to answer and then he said, "No. I'm originally from Arizona. The southern part."

"I took a trip with my mother to Tucson once. It's beautiful down there."

"Yes."

His one-word reply disappointed her. She'd hoped her remark would lead him to open up about his former home or something about his past life. But he wasn't going for it.

She went on. "But I happen to think our little area of the world right here is very pretty. Do you ever drive over to the lake?"

His brows pulled together. "You mean Lake Tahoe?"

She nodded and his frown grew deeper.

"No. I don't have any business over there."

Impatient now, she could barely keep from groaning out loud. Exactly where did he have business, she wanted to ask him. Were his interests confined to riding the range or in a dusty round pen, breaking a horse to ride?

She swallowed another bite of burger before she said, "Put like that, I and thousands more like me, also don't have any reason to go to Tahoe, except to enjoy the scenery. Jett and I have fond memories of the lake. When we were kids our father would often take us there for picnics." She sighed. "But that was before he took a permanent walk out of our lives."

Glancing across the table, she saw his blue eyes thoughtfully studying her face and immediately she could feel a rush of heat fill her cheeks.

"I don't recall your father ever visiting the ranch. And Jett never mentions him."

"It's been years since our father has been near Carson City. Once in a while I get a phone call from him. Or Jett will receive a letter in the mail. The last he heard, Dad was promising to come see his grandkids. So far that hasn't happened."

He looked confused. "So you still speak with your father?"

She smiled faintly. "Why not? We understand he's a wandering musician. If we'd tried to hold him here, he would've been miserable. And that wouldn't have done our mother or us kids much good. As long as he's playing in a band somewhere, he's happy. I think it took Jett a lot longer than me to accept our father's indifference. But having Sassy to love has made my brother look at things from a more understanding perspective. Some people just march to a different drummer and our father is one of them."

He reached for the bag of chips and poured a pile onto his plate. "Must be nice not to resent the man."

She shook her head. "I could never resent him. He was always a very loving man. He still loves us—in his own way. And that's what matters the most to me."

"It's clear we see things in a different way, Bella. If

I ever had the misfortune to run into my old man again, I'd take great pleasure in busting him in the mouth."

The hard bitter look on his face struck Bella far more than his words. The fact that he was harboring such anger and resentment toward anyone, much less his father, surprised her. Especially when she'd heard Jett describe how kindly and gently he treated every animal on the ranch. But she had to remember he'd not been as fortunate as she and Jett. They'd had a very loving mother, who'd worked hard to make sure her children had a normal home. From what Noah had told her, he'd not even had that much.

Not wanting to sound preachy, she simply said, "I'm sorry, Noah."

"Yeah. I'm sorry, too."

They finished the meal with only a few exchanges of small talk. Afterward, Bella helped him clear the table and wash what few dishes they'd used. As the two of them moved around the small space, an awkward tension began to build and she decided it was probably time for her to say goodbye.

With the last plate dried and put away in the cabinet, she folded the dish towel she'd been using and placed it on the end of the cabinet counter. "Thanks for the meal, Noah. I think I'd better be getting Casper back home before it gets dark."

She expected to see a look of relief cross his face. Instead, his expression remained stoic, making it impossible to discern his reaction to her announcement.

Who are you trying to kid, Bella? His reaction is as clear as a cloudless day. He could've offered you coffee or pointed out that the evening was still young, anything to invite you to stay longer. Face it, he's had all of your company he can stand.

Bella was trying to ignore the insulting voice going off in her head, when Noah said, "Right. It wouldn't do for you to meet up with a bear or mountain lion in the dark."

As far as Bella was concerned, he was much more dangerous to her well-being than any wild animal. Because she was drawn to him in ways she couldn't quite understand. She only knew that being in his presence quenched a need deep inside her.

She moved to the open doorway, then paused. "I keep a little bear bell tied to my saddle horn. The jingle helps ward away any predators." Now that she thought about it, the little tinkling bell was probably the sound that he'd heard when she'd first ridden up on Casper.

He hardly looked impressed by her safety measures, but he didn't say anything and Bella quickly stepped out of the cabin and walked over to Casper.

She was untying the get-down rope from the tree limb when she sensed Noah walking up behind her. The fact that he'd followed her out of the cabin surprised her and as soon as the rope fell loose, she turned a questioning look at him.

A frown was on his face and his gaze connected with hers for only a brief moment before it dropped to the ground. He said, "Before you go there's something I need to say."

Her heart was suddenly pounding with foolish hope. Maybe he had enjoyed her company after all, she thought. Maybe he was going to tell her he'd like to see her again.

"Yes?" she asked.

His gaze returned to hers and she gave him an encouraging smile.

He cleared his throat. "I—uh, just wanted to say it was nice having you here."

She couldn't remember the last time a man's words had filled her with such warm pleasure. "I enjoyed it very much, too, Noah."

A frown pulled his brows together and as he swiped a hand through his thick hair, it became clear to Bella that he was carefully trying to choose what he was going to say next. Could it be he was trying to decide how best to ask her out on a date? It was crazy how much she wanted that to happen.

Finally he said, "Look, Bella, you're a nice lady. And I have to be honest with you. I—well, I would appreciate it if you wouldn't do this again."

Certain she must have heard him wrong, her head moved stiffly back and forth. "This? What are you talking about?"

The confusion in her voice only seemed to frustrate him more and he raked a hand over his black hair as his eyes evaded meeting hers.

"Coming here to the cabin—my home."

The direct meaning of his words hit her so hard she felt like someone had whammed a fist to her stomach.

"Oh." Pain spread through her chest as she quickly turned back to Casper and began to tighten the saddle cinch. Oh, Lord, she'd made a giant fool of herself, but strangely that wasn't the reason for her pain. No, it was the fact that he was so callously rejecting her. "Guess I've made a pest of myself. Sorry."

She'd fastened the end of the latigo neatly in its holder and was backing the horse away from the tree in order to mount him, when Noah spoke again.

"It's not that, Bella. It's—just for the best. Can we leave it at that?"

She supposed she should have felt embarrassed. After all, she couldn't remember any time in her life when a man had so bluntly spurned her. Even Marcus with all his cheating and lies had vowed he loved her and had desperately tried to hang on to her. Even her old boss, who'd recently gotten married, had liked Bella as a person. But for some reason, Noah just flat-out wanted no part of her. The realization made her want to cry, or scream. She didn't know which. In the end she chose to do neither.

"Sure, Noah. You don't have to explain. I apologize for making a nuisance of myself and ruining your evening. Don't worry. It won't happen again."

Not daring to look at him, she crossed the split reins over Casper's neck and started to lift the toe of her boot to the stirrup when Noah's hand suddenly wrapped around her elbow.

Insulted even more, she shrugged his hold away. "Thank you," she said stiffly, "but I don't need help getting into the saddle."

To her surprise, he wrapped his hand around her upper arm and she twisted her head to look at him. His blue eyes were partially hidden beneath the scowl of his brows, but there was a fire, a glint of life in them that she'd not seen before.

"I know I'm not the sort of gentleman that you rub shoulders with, but I do have manners, Bella."

She'd never been a mean-spirited person, but she did have her pride, even though he was trying his best to crush it.

"Really?" she asked, her voice etched with sarcasm. "Well, if you had, good manners would have been telling me that you enjoyed my company—even though you didn't."

She expected him to drop his hold on her arm and move aside, but he clearly had other ideas. He tugged her around to face him and Bella's knees went weak as his steely blue gaze grabbed on to hers.

"Don't twist my words, Bella. I didn't say anything about not enjoying your company."

"But you just said—"

"I don't want you back up here. I know what I said. And I meant it."

No man had ever shaken Bella as much as Noah had at this very moment. There was something about his dark, brooding presence that reminded her of a stormy night, when shutters slammed and every shadow seemed to lurk with hidden dangers. And yet just to have him touch her was wildly exciting.

"Why?" she asked quietly.

"You little fool," he muttered. "Don't you have it figured out by now?"

"No. I—"

Before she could finish, he yanked her forward and straight into his arms. The shock caused her to drop her hold on Casper's rein and the horse moved a few steps away.

"Then I need to make it clear. I can't have you around me. Not when I want to do this."

She watched in fascination as his face dipped toward hers. Then his lips made contact with hers and instantly her eyes squeezed shut, her breath caught in her throat.

Noah was kissing her!

For a split second the fact was so shocking she couldn't think or react. Then just as quickly pleasure exploded inside her, causing her arms to wrap around his neck, the front of her body to press tightly against his.

Ever since he'd stopped on the side of the road to

help her, she'd been dreaming of kissing him, tasting his lips and having his strong arms wrapped around her. Now, reality was proving to be a thousand times more potent and far more delicious than anything she could've conjured up in her mind.

As the kiss went on, Bella could feel herself sinking into a pool of liquid pleasure and it didn't matter that she was in danger of losing her breath. She didn't want the bliss to end.

But just as suddenly as the kiss had started, it ended with Noah tearing his lips from hers. The break did little to stop her reeling senses and she was forced to hang on to his shoulders to steady herself.

"You see now why I can't have you near me?"

The gruff rasp of his voice caused her eyelids to flutter open and she found herself staring directly into his eyes. At the moment the blue orbs were dark and stormy, but whether that was a result of anger or passion, she couldn't tell.

"Oh, Noah," she whispered. "I—"

Before she could say anything else, he turned and moved a few steps from her. Bella wiped a shaky hand over her face, then walked over to stand at his side.

"I don't understand," she finally managed to say.

He let out a short, caustic laugh. "You think I do? Ever since I first laid eyes on you I've been wanting to do that. Stupid of me, huh?"

The trembling that had started on the inside of her during their kiss had now pushed its way to the outside, making her hands shake and her voice quaver. "I've been wanting to do that ever since I laid eyes on you, too. Does that make me stupid, too?"

A tight grimace twisted his features. "No. It makes you a liar."

Bella stepped in front of him and stabbed him with an angry look. "You can call me bold or forward or unladylike, but don't call me a liar. That's one thing I'm not."

"Then you must be a hypocrite. Jett says you had a crush on your old boss—that you still do. He's the one you've had ideas about kissing. Not me!"

Doing her best to hang on to her temper, she said, "Jett doesn't know what he's talking about. I never had a crush on Curtis. Not while I worked as a paralegal in his law office or after I left it. I admired him for many reasons and even thought he'd make a good husband— but I could see he wasn't meant for me."

Bella couldn't go on to explain that being around Curtis had never filled her head with erotic images. She'd never pictured herself making wild, passionate love to the man, the way she had with Noah. But those secret fantasies were far too intimate to share with this man.

Shaking his head, he glanced toward Casper, and Bella followed the direction of his attention. Thankfully the horse had been trained not to run away. At the moment he was happily tearing at the tufts of grass growing in scattered patches over the rocky ground.

"Forget I mentioned anything about the man," Noah muttered gruffly. "Who you have your eye set on is none of my business. Unless you try to make me your target. So before you make your play, you need to know that I'm not about to let anything develop between us. Not now. Not ever."

Bella proudly lifted her chin. "Then why did you kiss me?"

"That was my way of explaining the situation."

She refrained from rolling her eyes toward the treetops. "It sure didn't feel like a demonstration, explanation, or anything of the sort. It felt like an old-fashioned kiss—the kind two people with mutual attraction share. And if you could be totally honest with me, you'd admit that you want to do it again. I do."

His jaws clamped so tight Bella figured his back teeth were probably in danger of crumbling beneath the pressure.

Turning his gaze back to her, he said, "Bella, I'm sorry, but I don't have the luxury of playing games with the opposite sex. Especially when the games could become dangerous."

"I would've never guessed you could be such an ass, Noah Crawford," she said in a low, angry voice. "But I should've known. It's no wonder you live such a solitary life. There's no one around here worthy of your presence!"

With tears threatening to fall, she hurried over to Casper and swung herself into the saddle. Yet before she could kick the horse into a gallop, Noah was there, reaching up and dragging her out of the saddle.

Bella practically fell into his arms and she was forced to grab hold of his shoulders to keep from sliding down the front of his body.

She gasped with shock. "Noah! What—are you—doing?"

"I'm doing what both of us want!"

The words came out on a fierce growl and then he was kissing her again. Only this time the meeting of their mouths instantly turned into a frenetic search that lasted so long Bella was certain she was going to faint.

The rushing noise in her ears grew so loud she couldn't hear the wind or the birds or even the moans in her own throat. Then, just as her knees were about to buckle, he lifted his head, allowing her to suck in a reviving breath of oxygen. Yet before she could gather herself completely, he stepped back, removing the anchoring support of his shoulders.

Forced to grab on to the fender of Casper's saddle to keep from falling, she stared in shocked wonder at him.

"Noah, I—"

"Don't say anything else, Bella," he said in a husky growl. "Just go home. Before I say to hell with everything and carry you inside the cabin."

Shaking almost violently now, she followed his order and quickly swung herself onto Casper's back. The horse instantly sensed her turmoil and began to dance and shake his head against the bit. Without sparing a glance at Noah, she urged the animal into a gallop and didn't ease the pace until she was long gone from the cowboy's view.

Chapter Four

Three days later on a late Wednesday evening, Noah was in the barn, taking an inventory of the ranch's saddles and tack when a footstep behind him had him glancing over his shoulder.

The instant he spotted Jett striding toward him, he inwardly winced. This was the first time this week that he'd seen his boss. Any information they'd needed to share about ranch work had been done over the phone and Noah had been hoping by the time he faced Jett again, he would've forgotten all about his afternoon with Bella.

But so far Noah had found it impossible to get Bella, or the kisses they'd shared, out of his mind. From the moment she'd galloped Casper away from the cabin, his thoughts had been obsessed with the woman. Now he didn't know what to do to shake the misery he was carrying around inside him.

"Hey, Noah. I saw your truck and wondered what you were still doing here. It's getting late."

The tall, dark-haired man dressed in worn jeans, cowboy boots and a gray battered hat looked nothing like a lawyer, but Jett Sundell was a damned good one and an equally good rancher. Along with those attributes, he was a devoted husband and father and one of the best friends Noah had.

"Hello, Jett." He gestured toward a group of saddles the men used on a daily basis. "I was just going over our saddles. I'm afraid Reggie broke the tree in his today. He roped a bull and it jerked him and his horse over. The horn was literally buried in the ground. Now the whole damned thing is wiggling."

A look of concern crossed Jett's face. "Don't worry about replacing the saddle. I want to know about Reggie and the horse."

"They were lucky. I don't know how, but both came out of the spill unscathed. Reg got a lot of ribbing from the men, but he took it all with a laugh. I called Denver over at the Silver Horn to see if they had any used saddles for sale. He tells me they have a few. Most are pretty worn, but at least it would be a hell of a lot better than spending a couple of thousand for a new one."

Jett nodded. "I'll be working the Horn tomorrow. While I'm there I'll have a look at them. Rafe has all the using saddles for his men handmade, so whatever they have for sale will be good ones." He walked over and took a seat on an overturned feed bucket. "Sassy's been trying to locate some hay. I realize it's only the first part of May and we should have grass for a while, but what with the drought, she's concerned that by the time winter rolls around hay will be as scarce as hen's teeth. The alfalfa crops over in Churchill County are already sold and they're not even ready to cut yet."

"She's probably right. I figure the sooner we fill the barns, the better," Noah agreed.

Bending forward, Jett rested his forearms against his knees and looked over at Noah. "She found some timothy for sale, but the stuff is way up in Idaho and baled from last year's crop. I told her to keep searching. I don't want the cost of shipping that far. Especially when it's not fresh-cut."

"Don't worry," Noah told him. "It's early yet. Has she talked to Finn? The last I heard, her brother had his hay meadows producing. If he has surplus, he might sell what he doesn't need."

"You're right. I'll talk to Sassy about it tonight." Chuckling, he added, "That is, we'll talk after bath time, story reading and rocking Mason to sleep."

Of Jett and Sassy's three children, Mason was the baby of the bunch, born just before Thanksgiving last year. Noah was very fond of all three kids, but he couldn't deny he was particularly attached to little Mason. The dark-haired baby rarely uttered a cry and whenever he saw Noah, he always reached for him.

Mason would probably be the closest thing he ever had to having a son. The hollow thought had Noah moving restlessly over to a wall where a slew of bridles neatly hung on rows of nails. Automatically, he picked up a shiny pair of bits and worked the moving parts back and forth.

"You didn't see Bella around this afternoon, did you?" Jett asked.

Just hearing her name was like a punch in the gut and for a moment he gripped the bit so hard he very nearly bent the silver shank. "No. Why?"

"Just wondering," Jett replied. "She wrapped up her work early this afternoon and said she was coming home. I was hoping you might have seen her out riding. She hasn't been herself at all this week. I've been a bit worried about her."

Noah stared unseeingly at the wall of bridles as the last few minutes of Bella's visit to the cabin played over in his mind. Try as he might, he still didn't know what had prompted him to kiss her. Then like a crazy man, he'd pulled her off Casper and once his mouth had landed on hers, he'd lost all control. But then so had she. The memory of her soft, eager lips moving against his, the way her body had practically wrapped itself around his, still had the power to make his groin ache with need.

"—riding the canyon. Noah? Hello? Are you with me?"

Jett's voice finally penetrated his deep thoughts and with a mental curse at himself, he looked over at his friend.

"Sorry, Jett. I was thinking about something. What were you saying?"

Frowning at him, Jett rose from the makeshift seat. "There must be something in the air that's causing late spring fever or some sort of mild dementia. Bella's been going around the office in a fog. Now I can't even keep your attention. Are you all right?"

No. There was nothing right about him, Noah wanted to say. But he couldn't. How could he explain to Jett that he was overwhelmed with the need to make love to his sister? That every moment of the day, she was on his mind like a wide-awake dream? Not only that, his encounter with Bella was the very thing he'd desperately tried to avoid all these years he'd been on the J Bar S.

It was crazy. And he had to put a stop to it before his job, his whole life here on the ranch, came to an end.

"Hell, yes, I'm all right. Why wouldn't I be?" he asked gruffly.

Jett shrugged as he passed a keen gaze over Noah's face. "You tell me. You're not acting like your usual self. Have any of the guys been slacking or giving you a problem?"

"No. They're all working hard and no tempers have flared. I'm just tired, that's all. In fact, if there's nothing else we need to talk over, I'm going to head home."

"Go ahead. I figure Sassy's probably waiting dinner for me anyway." He moved closer and gave Noah an affectionate slap on the shoulder. "Don't pay any mind to me, Noah. It's just that I worry about you."

Noah was momentarily taken aback. It was true that Jett considered him more of a close friend than an employee, but he'd never expressed this kind of concern before. "Worry? Why would you do that?"

A wry expression crossed Jett's face. "Because I want you to be happy. And it's obvious that you aren't."

Ignoring the hollow pain in the pit of his stomach, Noah let out a mocking snort. "Since when did you become a psychiatrist?"

"I don't need a doctor's degree to figure out that much."

Noah hung the leather headstall back on its hook. "I guess the next thing you're going to do is tell me I need to get out more. Find myself a woman and have a passel of kids."

"Well, it wouldn't be the first time I've told you that."

"I wish to hell it would be your last."

"A family would change your life—for the better," Jett argued.

"Over my dead body," Noah muttered, then giving his hat an unnecessary tug onto his forehead, he started toward the door. "I'm going home."

"Noah, wait a minute."

Reluctantly, Noah paused and turned to face the other man. "Jett, I really don't want to get into this."

Jett shook his head. "I'm not about to give you a lecture, Noah, or anything like that. I just wanted to say that we've been good friends for years now. And I've never tried to stick my nose in your private life. Past or present. But it's always been clear to me that you're running and hiding from something. I just hope that one of these days you'll turn and face whatever it is that's haunting you. Because until then you'll just be going through the motions of living."

His jaw tight, Noah muttered, "If that isn't one of your lectures, I'd sure hate to hear one."

Grinning now, Jett made a backhanded wave at the door. "Go on. That's all I have to say about the matter. I'll call you from the Horn tomorrow and let you know about the saddles."

The sudden change of subject had Noah heaving out a breath of relief. "Fine. I'll see you tomorrow."

"Yeah. Have a good night, buddy."

Outside, Noah crossed the ranch yard to where his truck was parked near the saddling pen. By now darkness was fast approaching, shrouding the barns and connecting corrals with deep shadows. The rest of the ranch hands had left more than an hour ago and, other than a handful of goats eating from a trough, the work area was quiet.

At any other time Noah would have lingered to relish the peacefulness, but not tonight. He wanted to get away from Jett and the sight of his happy home lit with warm lights. In a few minutes, when Jett walked through the door, the kids would fling themselves at him and Sassy would no doubt greet him with a kiss.

Noah didn't know what that might feel like. To have a family shower him with such love. And he'd probably never know. Because he wasn't ever going to put his trust, or his well-being, in the hands of a woman. No matter how sweet her kisses were.

The drive to Noah's cabin took fifteen minutes, not because there were several miles between the two places, but rather the road was rough, making it slow traveling. As Noah maneuvered the truck over the rub-board surface, he tried once again to clear his mind of Bella, but she remained stubbornly fixed in his thoughts.

Jett had said he was worried about his sister and Noah couldn't help but wonder if her behavior had anything to do with last Sunday and her visit to the cabin. Or was he putting too much importance on those hot kisses they'd shared?

Damn it, he'd not wanted to insult her or hurt her. God help him, she was the only woman he'd ever felt the need to cherish and protect. That's why he'd said those cutting things to her, because she deserved much better than him. He'd thought his bluntness would show her he wasn't a man who was worthy of her. She needed to understand that he was only a cowboy with nothing to offer her. Nothing at all. And yet, these past few days, he'd been overwhelmed with the longing to see her face again, to hear her voice and feel her soft lips yielding to his.

As he neared the turnoff to Bella's place, he told himself he wasn't even going to look in her direction. But that all changed when he spotted a light flickering through the pines and realized it was coming from Bella's barn.

If she was having trouble with one of the horses and needed help, she could call Jett. But he had a feeling she wouldn't want to disturb her brother's evening, unless it was absolutely necessary. No, she'd try to deal with the problem herself before she asked for help.

With a groan of self-disgust, he wrenched the wheel at the last moment and steered the truck onto her driveway.

Bella was walking up the alleyway of the barn when she spotted the headlights sweeping in front of the open doorway. At this time of evening Jett was usually having dinner with his family and none of her friends in town had mentioned they might drive out for a visit. She couldn't imagine who the unexpected caller might be.

She quickened her stride, while dusting bits of alfalfa hay from the front of her shirt and jeans. By the time she reached the front entrance, she spotted a man walking toward her. His hat was sitting low on his forehead, making it impossible to see his face, but there was no mistaking the tall, muscled body or that long easy walk.

Noah!

Without even realizing it, her heels dug into the soft earth, bringing her to an abrupt halt just inside the doorway.

He quickly closed the last few steps between them and all at once a familiar trembling began to consume her entire body.

"What are you doing here?" she asked bluntly. "Has something happened to Jett or his family?"

"Nothing is wrong. I saw your light in the barn and

thought something might be wrong with one of the horses."

If she had any backbone at all, she would tell him to get lost. That she would rather crawl on her belly before she asked for his help. But she'd never been a vindictive person. Besides, how could she send him away when everything inside of her was jumping with crazy joy at the sight of him?

"You have a cell phone," she said flatly. "Why didn't you call Jett and ask him to check on me?"

His lips thinned to a straight line and as Bella studied his rigid features, she wondered why his kiss had tasted so incredibly good. And why, after days of fighting with herself, she couldn't get it or him out of her mind.

"He doesn't need the bother."

Her boots planted in a wide stance, she folded her arms over her breasts. "You think I'm just a bother, period. Don't you?"

His nostrils flared. "Do you need any help?"

She relaxed her stance. "I'm not having any sort of problem. I was simply down here visiting."

The annoyance on his face turned to one of confusion and he glanced over her shoulder, toward the back of the barn. "Visiting? Is someone else down here with you?"

She laughed. "No. Just the horses. I was grooming them and giving them a few treats. They're very good listeners. Did you know that?"

"I try to listen to mine. Not the other way around."

She smiled faintly. "No. I don't expect you ever need to talk to anyone. Not even your horse."

"You don't know what I need," he muttered.

Even though the overhead lighting in the barn was dim, she could see his brooding gaze traveling over her and Bella wondered if he still had the urge to kiss her. Or had he gotten that weakness out of his system?

"Apparently, you don't either," she retorted.

"I need to be left alone," he said stiffly. "I know that much."

Shaking her head, she stepped toward him. "Seems to me that you've had that for seven years. After that length of time you ought to be the happiest man on the planet."

"Maybe I am, Bella. So if you don't need my help, I'll be on my way."

He turned to go, but she quickly caught his arm. "Noah, wait."

His gaze scanned her face, then dropped pointedly down to the hand she'd curled around his forearm. "Why?" he asked simply.

Once again she could feel herself trembling, her heart pounding. He was like a drug, she decided. One that entered her bloodstream the moment she laid eyes on him. "I—because I wanted to thank you for stopping. I'm grateful that you cared enough to offer your help."

He glanced away from her. "It was stupid of me. You don't need a man's help. Especially mine."

Even though his remark was cutting, at least it gave her a glimpse of how he actually viewed her.

"What gave you that idea?" she asked.

He didn't answer immediately and about the time she'd decided he was going to ignore her question completely he turned his attention back to her.

"You're a successful career woman, Bella."

Reluctant to remove her hand from his arm, she left it there, relishing the warmth of the hard muscle beneath her fingers. "I see. So that makes everything easy for me."

"Something like that."

Her short laugh was full of disbelief, but she didn't expand on the matter. This chance meeting with him was too precious to have an argument cut it short.

"I have supper on the stove," she told him. "If you've not eaten yet, I'd like for you to join me."

He started to pull his arm away, but she tightened her hold on him.

"I can't. My clothes and boots are nasty."

"I like you just the way you are. Tells me you've been working. Besides, I owe you a meal." She dropped his arm and stepped over to where a light switch was situated on the wall. After flipping it off, she said, "I've already put the horses back in the pasture. So if you'll help me shut the doors, we'll be on our way."

To her relief he didn't put up any more argument and after the double doors on the barn were secured, they walked side by side along a path outlined with solar footlights.

At the back of the house, they entered the kitchen, where Bella went straight to the sink and began to wash her hands.

"Hang your hat and make yourself at home," she tossed over her shoulder. "You know where the bathroom is."

When she heard no movement behind her, she looked over her shoulder to see him standing in the middle of the room. His hat was clutched in both hands and from the look on his face, bolting was the main thing on his mind.

"Is anything wrong?" she asked.

He raked fingers through his flattened hair and two pieces fell onto a black eyebrow. "Bella, didn't you hear anything I said the other evening?"

With her back to him, she dried her hands on a paper towel. "Yes. I heard everything you said. But that doesn't mean I'm going to follow your orders."

"I said some nasty things to you."

"Yes, you did," she agreed. "But I've already forgiven you. Besides, you were only trying to make me dislike you."

She heard his footsteps come up behind her and it was all she could do to keep from turning and sliding her arms around his waist. She wanted to rest her cheek upon his chest, to smell his skin, feel his breath upon her hair and the warmth of his body seeping into hers.

"Bella, why are you making this so hard for me?"

His voice was soft and the sound caressed her like gentle fingers on her skin.

She turned to face him and the anguish and need she saw churning in the blue depths of his eyes touched her as nothing had before.

Swallowing at the tightness in her throat, she said gently, "Noah, I'm not trying to make you miserable. I enjoy your company and I think you enjoy mine. I'm not asking you for anything. Just a bit of your time. What can be wrong with that?"

"All right," he surrendered. "As long as you know there can be nothing between us—nothing serious, that is. I guess it won't hurt for us to be friends."

Joyous relief poured through her and she gave him a wide smile. "Friends, yes! Now you go on and wash up while I get our meal ready. I hope you like beef stew."

He gave her a half smile, yet Bella felt as though he'd just given her the moon.

"Sure. I like it just fine."

She watched him leave the room, then sped over to the stove and switched a flame on under the pot of stew.

Noah was staying! Her heart kept singing the words over and over as she set the table, fetched crackers from the pantry and heated cornbread muffins in the microwave.

Have you lost your mind, Bella? Just because Noah is going to eat a bowl of stew with you doesn't mean it's time to get all dreamy-eyed and sappy in the head. The man said he'd be friends. And you can bet your bottom dollar that's all he'll ever be to you. So why bother? Why are you feeling all this silly romantic joy? It's only going to hurt you later on.

The voice going off in her head was something she'd been fighting ever since she'd discovered Marcus had been having affairs. Each time she'd let herself look at a man or dream of having a family, it reminded her how he'd shattered her trust, her whole future. But time had helped heal the hurt she'd endured from her cheating ex-husband. Oh, she still had scars from the ordeal, but she was determined not to let Marcus ruin any more of her life. It was time to let herself hope and love and plan again.

By the time Noah returned to the kitchen, she had everything set out on the table except for their drinks.

"I have a pitcher of iced tea, but if you'd rather have beer, I think I have one in the refrigerator," she told him.

"The tea will be fine."

She poured their drinks. "Everything is ready. Let's eat."

He helped her into the long bench, then took a seat at the other place setting. All the while, Bella could hardly keep her eyes off him. This evening he was wearing a white Western shirt made of heavy cotton. Since his trip from the bathroom, he'd rolled the long sleeves back on his forearms and his dark skin made a vivid contrast next to the shirt. His damp hair was smoothed back from his forehead and lay in curling tendrils at the back of his neck. Just looking at his rough, rugged exterior practically took her breath away.

"So how did your day go?" she asked as she ladled thick stew into a bowl and passed it over to him.

"Busy. We moved cattle from Sage Meadow over to Salt Lick Flats. Reggie took a spill on his horse but thankfully he and the horse are okay."

"That's good. I'm sure you know that Reggie and his wife have a new baby girl. It would be especially awful for him to be hurt now."

"Yeah. His wife has been pretty fragile ever since the baby was born, so I think Reg has been having to shoulder a lot of the household chores at home, along with his work on the ranch."

"Oh, I wasn't aware Evita was having problems. I should pay her a visit and see if I can help in some way."

He looked at her. "You'd do that?"

His surprise put a frown on her face. "Why wouldn't I? Reg is a part of our ranch family. And I know Evita well. I'll make a point to go by their place tomorrow."

He didn't say anything as he began to eat and Bella wondered why it surprised him that she'd want to help a friend. True, he didn't really know her, but surely he could see she wasn't a snob or self-absorbed person.

You're a successful career woman.

He'd stated the fact as though that set her above other women and made men an unnecessary part of her life. She could only hope he'd give her the chance to show him how wrong his thinking was.

"Jett told me you left work early today."

Her spoon paused halfway to her mouth. "Jett was talking to you about me?"

He didn't look across the table at her. Instead, he focused on the bowl of stew and the muffin in his hand. "He's a little concerned about you. That's all."

Before she'd left the office this afternoon, Jett had asked her why she'd been moping about all week. Bella hadn't been able to tell him the truth of the matter. That she'd been miserable over her argument with Noah. Unless Noah had mentioned their little Sunday dinner to Jett, then her brother didn't even know she'd been with the ranch foreman, much less that she'd been kissing him.

She broke off a piece of muffin and slathered it with butter. "I'm fine. I wrapped up a trial case this morning and the rest of the work on my desk can wait until Monday, so I decided to close up shop and come home."

"To go riding?" he asked.

Bella shook her head. "I considered it. But I ended up staying here in the kitchen instead."

A few moments of silence passed as they continued to eat. Finally, he said, "This is good. Where did you learn to cook? From your mother? Or do you watch all those cooking shows on television?"

She chuckled. "How do you know about cooking shows? You don't have a television."

"So you noticed. You must think I'm really eccentric."

She could have told him that she'd noticed everything about him and his modest home. Moreover, she'd spent these past few days thinking of little else.

"Not really. Actually, I'm a little envious. Sometimes I wish I could do away with every technical gadget I own. The contraptions intrude not only on our privacy, but also upon a person's life."

"But the convenience is nice," he reasoned. "When

I'm out somewhere on the ranch and need to make a call to Jett or someone, I don't have to ride all the way into the ranch yard to reach a phone. That is, if the signal is strong enough for my cell phone to work."

She nodded. "When Jett first got the ranch from our grandparents, there wasn't even a phone in the house. Now he has a little office inside the barn, complete with a landline and internet access. The ranch has changed so much these past few years. And mostly because Sassy became a part of Jett's life."

"Hmm. I've not forgotten the first day Jett went to pick her up at the airport. Instead of taking her to the hotel room she'd already reserved, he brought her here to the ranch."

Bella chuckled. "That's right. And she's been here ever since. At that time none of us knew she was actually Orin Calhoun's daughter. I think it still shocks her to think she's part of such a wealthy family."

He grunted mockingly. "There's no chance of that happening to me. I know for a fact which side of the track I came from."

She thoughtfully stirred her stew. "Sassy came from very humble beginnings. You know, her adoptive parents perished in a fire when she was just a young teenager. Being wealthy was never her plan. All she ever wanted was a family. And I have a feeling you wouldn't ever want to be that wealthy—I mean the Calhoun kind of wealth."

He shook his head. "I don't need to be rich. Not that way."

"Lucky for Jett you feel that way or you wouldn't be content to work here. You'd have a ranch somewhere of your own."

A shuttered look came over his face as he reached to

dip himself another helping of stew from the iron pot sitting in the middle of the table.

"I'd never want a place of my own," he said.

The sudden sharpness to his voice told her she'd somehow stepped onto sensitive territory.

"Oh. Well, Jett has said he gives you a part of the calf crop every year as a bonus and you've never sold a one of them. That gave me the idea you might be saving them to put on your own land."

The corners of his lips tightened. "You believe that's what defines a man? What he owns?"

Confused by the abrupt change in his attitude, she frowned. "Not what he owns, Noah, but rather what he does."

He said nothing and Bella could see he wasn't at all convinced she was expressing how she really felt on the subject.

Holding back a sigh, she picked up her glass and leaned back in her chair. "When Marcus and I first got married he and his two brothers worked for their father's asphalt company. Marcus located jobs and arranged the contracts. The position paid well and he never had to dirty his hands."

"Some men are just lucky."

She sipped the sweet tea, while wondering where she'd found the courage to talk about Marcus. He was a subject she didn't care to share with anyone. After all, he was a constant reminder that she'd not used good judgment. But something about Noah seemed to open doors inside of her and everything came rushing out.

"Marcus certainly didn't see it that way. He was constantly harping to me that his family wasn't giving him the respect or appreciation he deserved. Eventually, he quit and tried to cobble together his own highway construction business."

A cynical groove marked his cheek. "You can't blame a guy for wanting to be independent."

"I understood that part of it. But Marcus was too young and inexperienced to jump into such an endeavor. He borrowed a lot of money, lost it and somehow managed to borrow more. But by that point our marriage was on the rocks."

His lips slanted with disapproval. "So is that why you divorced him? Because his business failed?"

She shook her head. "His business didn't fail. After the shaky beginning it started making money. Quite a lot, in fact. But the money, or the fact that he was his own boss, wasn't important to me. I would've much rather had a husband who considered honesty and fidelity more important than his ego."

He looked at her. "So you divorced him because he was a cheater?"

Blowing out a heavy breath, she placed her glass back on the table and picked up her spoon. "That's right. I've spent a lot of sleepless nights wondering what it was about me that was missing and what Marcus had been searching for in all those other women. The only answer I could ever come up with was that I wasn't woman enough to keep him faithful." Smiling faintly, she glanced across the table at him. "But that's all over with."

His blue gaze made a long survey of her face and Bella realized that ever since they'd entered the house, she'd not even bothered to glance in the mirror. No doubt her hair was mussed and her makeup had faded away hours ago. But she liked to think that Noah was a man who looked beyond the surface. She only hoped he couldn't see all the scars and doubts she carried. More than anything she wanted him to think she was brave and strong and worthy of his attention.

"Is it really?" he asked.

Did he actually care? Or was she reading too much into the simple question?

"Truly."

"That's good," he said softly, "because you should never think of yourself as lacking."

Coming from any other man, she would take those words with a grain of salt. But coming from Noah made them mean something.

"Thank you, Noah," she said huskily, then feeling a bit like a blushing teenager, she quickly rose from the table and crossed over to the cabinet counter. "Please keep eating. I'm just going to put some coffee on to brew. It will go good with dessert."

"You have dessert?"

The faint surprise in his voice caused her to chuckle. "Unfortunately, I have an insatiable sweet tooth, so I'm baking all the time. Even when I'm swamped with work, I somehow manage to throw something in the oven. Tonight I have peach cobbler. Made with fresh California peaches. So you might want to save a little room for a dish of it."

"I'll try to make room for it," he said.

But would he ever make room in his heart for her?

Is that what you want, Bella? For Noah to love you? The man is carrying a load of baggage. If he ever knew about loving anyone, somewhere along the way, he's forgotten it all. Is that the kind of man you want to hang your feelings and hopes on?

Prompted by the questions going on in her head, Bella glanced over her shoulder at him. From where she stood, she couldn't see his face. But the sight of his proud dark head and the strength of his broad shoulders was all it took to convince her that she wanted him in her life.

He insisted they could only be friends. But she had to believe that sooner rather than later, she could prove to him that they could be much, much more.

Chapter Five

Minutes later, after they'd finished the stew and Noah had helped her clear the table, Bella suggested they take dessert to the living room.

"My jeans and boots are too grimy for that," he told her. "Let's go out on the back porch. The night has probably cooled by now."

"Sounds good to me," she agreed. "I'll put everything on a tray."

Noah stood to one side, watching her dish up bowls of cobbler and fill two cups with coffee.

She did everything with a simple grace that was both charming and sexy and Noah couldn't deny that being near her was like sitting in front of a warm fire on a cold night. It not only filled him with pleasure, it soothed the empty holes inside him. He'd never thought any woman could affect him that much. And especially not a woman like Bella, who was clearly cut from a better piece of cloth.

Noah figured he should be feeling guilty or stupid for accepting her invitation for supper. But he couldn't. For the first time in years, he actually felt like smiling.

Seeing she was about to pick up the tray, he moved in and pushed her hands aside. The moment his fingers brushed against hers, she paused to look up at him and Noah's gaze instantly dropped to her lips.

From the moment he'd walked up to her at the barn this evening, he'd been aching to kiss her, to find out for himself if all that passion he remembered had been real or exaggerated. But he couldn't kiss her. He'd sworn they could only be friends. And for his sake and hers, he had to stick to his promise.

Clearing his throat, he said, "I'll carry it. You get the door."

With a faint nod, she stepped around him and headed to the door. Noah followed her onto the porch where she switched on a lamp near a long wicker couch.

A low coffee table was positioned in front of the couch so Noah placed the tray on it. A few steps away, Bella rubbed both hands up and down her upper arms. "It has gotten rather cool. I think I'd better go grab a sweater. Make yourself comfortable and I'll be right back."

She went into the house and Noah sat down on the far end of the couch. While he waited for her to return, he glanced around the long porch and suddenly found himself thinking back to another time when he'd sat on a ground level porch made of rock and gazed out at the rough, ragged hills of southern Arizona. He and Ward, the owner of the Verde Canyon Ranch, had often sat together in the late evenings, sipping coffee and talking over the day's work.

The two men had always had plenty to talk about. With Verde Canyon covering several thousand acres, there'd always been something to be done, cattle to be tended, horses to be trained and fences to be mended. *Verde Canyon.* It was the only place he'd ever truly called home and he'd expected to live there until the day he died. But even the best-laid plans could be torn apart. Now he was just grateful that he'd found Jett and could make his home, such as it was, here on the J Bar S. At least here, his head wasn't filled with dreams and hopes and plans. No, those had all died on the Verde. And that's where they were buried.

"Sorry about that, Noah. You should've started without me."

Bella's voice interrupted his deep thoughts and he looked around to see her taking a seat on the opposite end of the couch. She'd wrapped a lacy shawl around her shoulders and loosened her ponytail. Now the dark waves settled around her shoulders like a silky cloud. His fingers itched to touch it, to lift it to his nose and breathe in the scent that was uniquely hers.

"I needed the extra time to let all that stew settle," he said. "I honestly don't know how I can hold another bite."

With a soft laugh, she said, "Well, you don't have to eat all the cobbler just to prove you like it."

She handed him one of the dessert bowls, then placed a coffee mug where he could easily reach it.

"Thanks."

He settled back and began to eat and Bella did the same.

After a long stretch of silence, she said, "The moon looks beautiful shining through the pines. The coyotes must like it. I can hear them howling down in the canyon."

"I hear them, too. Another reason why you shouldn't ride down there alone. You never know when you might run into a hungry pack of them."

She shook her head as though she considered his warning far-fetched. "Have you always been so overly protective?"

Only about you, Bella. Even though the words whispered through his head, he managed to bite them back before they could pass his lips. "No. I was an adventurous kid, always picking up snakes and lizards. I'd roam the hills outside the little town where we lived. I was always hoping I'd find a herd of javelina or a mountain lion."

"Did you go alone?"

He'd always been alone. At least, it had always felt that way to him. "Most of the time. My friends were too afraid of getting into trouble with their parents to go with me."

Even though he wasn't looking at her directly, he could feel her thoughtfully studying him. That was something different for Noah. The rare times he was with a woman she might look at him with amusement or even lust. But none ever studied him as though she was interested in the man beneath the surface. The notion that Bella saw him differently left him feeling restless and very vulnerable.

"Did your parents know where you were or what you were doing?" she asked.

His short laugh was a brittle, hollow sound. "They didn't care. They were more concerned about fighting over money or booze, or the one junky car they owned."

"I'm sorry. That must've been tough."

Sometimes in the quiet of the night, Noah could still hear the yelling and banging, the threats and tears. Back then, no matter where he'd tried to hide in the house, the violent sounds would reach him. Now after all these years, he still couldn't outrun the memories.

"It could've been worse. They never laid a mean hand on me." He stared out at the pines and the patches of silvery moonlight on the ground. "As a very small boy, I can remember my mother being very loving to me. She made me feel wanted and protected. But something changed, I didn't know what. Except that my parents had started fighting. After that, she began to push me away. Finally, she left and never came back."

"Hmm. That's odd that she didn't take you with her when she left."

Surprised by Bella's comment, he looked over at her. "Why do you say that? It was obvious she didn't want me around."

She shook her head. "You don't know that for sure. She clearly loved you once and a mother just doesn't stop loving her child. And she sure doesn't abandon it. She might have had emotional issues and figured you'd be better off without her. Or she could've been afraid. Your dad might have used you as a threat against her."

"No. Mom wasn't afraid for herself," he reasoned. "She stood up to him like a bulldog terrier."

She leaned forward and returned her bowl to the tray. "You don't understand, Noah. I didn't mean she was afraid for her own safety. I have the feeling she was trying to protect you. Believe me, in my line of work I see it all the time. Women make bad choices and then they become so afraid they make even worse choices. Your mother probably ran off because she didn't know any other way to handle the situation."

Noah had never thought in those terms. As a teenager he'd carried around the bitter hurt of being abandoned and that feeling had never left. Now Bella expected him to see things in a different light.

A sardonic smile twisted his lips. "Do you always look at things through rosy glasses? I thought you had to be a hard-nosed cynic to be a lawyer."

Chuckling, she touched a fingertip to her nose. "Oh, it doesn't feel that hard to me," she joked, then her expression turned serious. "Have you ever tried to locate your mother?"

A spot deep inside him squeezed so hard it caused his fingers to curl into his palms. "No. I don't even know if she's still alive."

"I have connections," she said. "I could make a search for you. No charge, of course."

"Bella, think about what you're asking," he said gently. "I've been doing fine like I am. What would it accomplish if you found her?"

"Have you ever thought she might need you?"

Her question should've had him bursting out with laughter. The notion that Margo Crawford might need her son was certainly absurd. And yet Noah couldn't feel any humor.

"No. I've never thought about it. And I don't intend to."

She seemed to accept his response because she didn't say anything else on the matter. In fact, she didn't say anything for a long time and Noah decided he didn't like her silence. Even when she was saying things that provoked him into thinking and feeling things he'd rather forget, he still enjoyed the sound of her voice and the idea that she wanted to connect herself with him through conversation.

After several more moments stretched in silence, he said, "Your parents obviously had their differences. Did they do a lot of loud arguing—fighting?"

She shook her head. "Not at all. I know that sounds odd, but you have to understand that my dad was, and I'm sure still is, one of those gentle souls that wouldn't raise his voice to anyone. Mom always said it was impossible to have an argument with Dad because he was always so kind and loving with her and us kids. I guess what I'm trying to say is that the memories of when our family was whole are very happy ones."

"You're lucky."

"I know that, Noah. In my work, I see far too many torn families."

Releasing a heavy breath, he looked away from her. "Yeah. I imagine you do."

He finished the last of his coffee, then before he could talk himself into remaining with her for a few minutes longer, he rose to his feet.

"Thanks for the meal, Bella. It's getting late, so I'll say good-night."

She quickly got to her feet. "Just a minute and I'll get your hat for you."

Noah knew better than to follow her back into the kitchen. Not when he wanted to find any excuse to pull her into his arms.

He waited at the door of the screened-in porch, until she emerged from the kitchen, carrying his hat. With a quick thank-you, he took it from her and levered it low on his forehead.

"I'll walk you to your truck," she said as she tied the shawl she was wearing into a knot between her breasts.

"That isn't necessary."

"I never said it was."

She moved past him, through the porch door and down the steps to leave Noah with no other choice but to follow.

As they walked along the footpath toward the barn, neither of them said anything and Noah could only wonder what she was thinking, wanting, feeling, and why any of that should matter to him.

Once they reached his truck, she stood no more than a step away and her flowery scent mingled with that of the nearby pines.

She said, "I'm glad you stopped to check on me, Noah. And I'm especially glad you decided to stay."

His hand rested on the door handle, but he couldn't bring himself to trip the latch. "I hadn't planned on it," he admitted.

"Why did you stay?" she asked.

His gaze left the shadows beyond her, to focus on her face. "I'm not exactly sure," he muttered, then shook his head. "That's not the truth. I stayed because I wanted to. Because I'm a glutton for punishment, I suppose."

She frowned. "So you consider spending time with me punishment?"

"If I let myself get involved with you it will be. We both know nothing good could come of it. Our worlds don't fit. We'd only end up hurting each other."

She moved closer and he drew in a sharp breath as her palm came to rest against the middle of his chest.

"Why wouldn't we fit together?" she asked softly. "I know what you are and you know what I am. There wouldn't be any surprises."

She made it sound so simple and tempting.

"Look, Bella, I'm not a family man," he said huskily. "Hell, I wouldn't know how to be. And that's what you need. Not someone like me."

She brought the other hand up to join the one already lying on his chest and Noah wondered how so much heat could radiate from her palms. Fire was flashing from his face all the way down to his groin.

"I need a man in my life before I can ever think about having a family," she reasoned.

"I'm not that man. And I can't ever be."

She opened her mouth to contradict him, but he didn't give her the chance.

He said, "All that stuff I told you tonight about my childhood, that's only a part of my past."

"Most everyone has things in their past they're not proud of, Noah. Me included. It's your future that I'm interested in."

He grimaced. "God willing, my future life won't look any different than it does right now."

"So you always want to live alone? You don't want a wife or children?"

"No. A wife and kids deserve someone who can give them love and devotion and make them happy. I can't even make myself happy."

She moved closer and Noah swallowed hard as the front of her body nestled itself against his.

"Perhaps that's because you haven't tried," she said, her voice barely above a whisper.

Like a single mound of sand trying to hold back an angry sea, the will to keep his hands off her suddenly crumbled. He wrapped them around her shoulders and pressed his fingers into her soft flesh.

"I've been trying to tell you, Bella, that we can only be friends. I've been trying to—"

"Reject me. Yes, that's obvious." She slid her hands upward until her fingers were touching the exposed flesh between the parted folds of his shirt. "But I don't think you really want to do that."

He reached out and gently traced his fingertip over the slant of her cheekbone. Her skin was as smooth as cream and he had no doubt it would taste just as rich.

His throat tightened as the urge to kiss her, make love to her began to tie his muscles into knots. "No. That's not what I want to do, Bella. But then you already know what you're doing to me. I imagine that makes you feel pretty damn good, doesn't it? Knowing you can make a big man like me weak in the knees."

Her eyes narrowed and then her head shook back and forth. "Why would you think such a thing? I have no desire to wield power over you. Or anyone else for that matter. That's one of the reasons I like being a lawyer. Because I believe everyone should be on equal ground."

"Well, in my case—"

"In your case, Noah, you're thinking too much. Worrying too much. Why can't you simply let yourself feel?"

"Because I'm feeling things that aren't good for me."

Slipping her arms around him, she nestled her cheek against the middle of his chest. The gesture of trust melted the cold chunk of reasoning inside him and without thinking, he stroked a hand over her dark hair.

A soft sigh slipped past her lips to mingle with the sound of the whispering pines. "After Marcus upended my world, I didn't think I'd ever want another man. Instead of thinking forward, I kept thinking in the past and all that I'd lost." She lifted her head and looked up at him. "But I'm beginning to see how that mindset was cowardly and stupid. I want more for myself than just wishing and hoping that things could be different."

"I'm not afraid, Bella. I'm practical." And that sensible side of him had kept him very cautious around any woman he met. If by some miracle he ever decided to take a wife, she needed to be cut from the same tough rawhide as himself. Not delicate lace, like Bella.

She said, "Being practical has no connection to falling in love. I might get hurt all over again. But so be it. I have to try to reach for my hopes and dreams."

Her words were like a battering ram, pounding at the door to his heart. Inch by inch he could feel the protective barrier caving and the fear that she might actually break through had him thrusting her gently away from him.

"Then you'd better go try to find all those dreams with another man," he said roughly.

A crushed expression momentarily froze her features and then her jaw went firm and resolute.

"Yes, I think I should do just that."

She turned and began walking back to the house. Noah stared after her, while telling himself he was doing the right thing. She would eventually find a good man to love. Yet even as he was struggling to convince himself, the image of some other man kissing her, holding her, making passionate love to her hit him like an avalanche.

Jealousy, or something much deeper, pushed him to go after her and in three long strides, his hand was on her shoulder, halting her steps.

"Noah, what—"

Whatever she was going to ask halted as he yanked her into his arms and brought his mouth down on hers. At first there was no response in her, but after one long second her lips parted and with a low groan, she flung her arms around his neck. Her reaction fueled the desperation and hunger that had gripped him from the moment she'd placed her hands on his chest and he crushed her body tight against his, while his tongue thrust past her teeth and into the warm cavern beyond.

Like a leaf sucked into a whirlwind, his senses spun in a vicious circle until he lost all thought. Nothing mattered but the pleasure that was pouring from his head to his toes, filling up every empty spot with soft, warm emotions he'd never felt before.

But the need for air finally forced him to lift his head and he opened his eyes to see she was gazing up at him, her expression dazed and confused.

"What does this mean, Noah?" she asked in a soft, husky voice. "You just told me to go find some other man."

"Damn it, I don't know what anything means anymore! But I'm certain about one thing—I don't want you with another man." His hands slipped down her back until his palms were cupping the fullness of her bottom. "Not like this."

"Noah."

His name came out on a soft breath and when her hands gently cradled his face, the notion that she could consider him as something precious was all it took for unbridled emotions to swell his chest and tighten his throat.

"I can't make you promises, Bella."

"I don't expect any. I'm just asking you not to put a wall between us."

Sighing, he lifted his gaze from her face to the dark shadows surrounding them. "You have your sights set on the wrong man, Bella. But you'll figure that out sooner rather than later."

Her warm body stirred against him and heat burned

like red hot coals in the pit of his belly. If he listened to his body instead of his head, he'd lead her straight into the house and make love to her. But he wasn't brave enough to take that reckless leap. He understood that once he took Bella to his bed, there would be no turning back. No chance to catch himself before the fall.

"I think I should warn you that I'm rarely wrong."

Her smile was a light in the darkness and Noah could resist it no more than a drink of cool water on a hot day.

"We'll see," was all he could manage to say before he bent his head and sought her mouth again.

This time he kept the kiss brief. Even so, just having her lips next to his was enough to leave him shaken and wanting more.

"I have to go, Bella."

"Are you sure?"

Her whispered question made it clear she was inviting him into her bedroom and into her life. The idea was beyond tempting, but thankfully it was also just scary enough to give him the strength to ease her out of his arms.

He let out a long breath. "Yeah. Sure."

"When will I see you again?"

"I can't say. We'll be busy moving cattle all next week. I'll try to stop by one evening on my way home."

She smiled again. "Okay. Unless something keeps me late at the office, I'll be here."

"Good night, Bella."

Before his resolve could crumble, he walked straight to his truck. But once he started the engine and turned the vehicle toward his cabin, the headlights swept across the backyard to illuminate Bella's silhouette. She was standing where he'd left her and now as she watched him pull away, she lifted a hand in farewell.

Pain squeezed the middle of his chest and as he drove the short distance to his place, he wondered how this thing with Bella had happened and exactly what he was going to do about it.

Chapter Six

By the time the middle of the work week rolled around, Bella had acquired three more cases to her already busy schedule. Two involved women seeking divorces, both from very wealthy husbands. The third was a young man accused of stealing valuable jewelry from a home where he was employed as a gardener.

Normally, Bella didn't deal in criminal cases. Nor did her brother, Jett. Both siblings usually focused on family law. But in this instance, the accused was the brother of an old schoolmate of Bella's and she'd not been able to turn away from her friend's plea for help.

Rising from her desk, she left the small room that made up her office and into an area where a young Hispanic woman sat typing at her desk.

Pepita Alvarez, better known as Peta to all her friends, acted as secretary to both Jett and Bella, which made the woman's workload enormous. Yet each time

Bella or Jett made noises about hiring more help for her, the young woman insisted she could handle the job on her own. Bella marveled at her efficiency.

As her shadow crossed Peta's desk, the black-haired beauty looked up. "Oh, Ms. Sundell, I didn't hear you. Do you need something?"

Bella smiled. "I was just wondering if Jett has anyone with him right now."

"No. I think Mr. Taylor left a few minutes ago. That was his last appointment for the day."

Bella chuckled. Mr. Taylor was an eccentric old man, who gave Jett fits by wanting to make changes in his will nearly every week. Her brother had finally given up on reasoning with the man. Instead, he merely followed Mr. Taylor's wishes and sent him a bill for services rendered.

"I wonder what changes he wanted made to his will today?" Bella mused out loud. "Bet the five thousand to his cat won't change."

Pepita shook her head. "Last week he wanted to make sure his twelve chickens went to his granddaughter. Poor old man. He's a hypochondriac. He believes he's going to die any minute."

"If that were to happen, Jett would really miss him. Not to mention the old man is contributing to the college funds for Jett's kids." She gave the secretary a conspiring wink. "I'll go see if he survived the meeting."

Her brother's office was located on the left side of the building and, like Bella's, had a picture window overlooking a busy street of Carson City. Up until a few years ago, Jett had worked exclusively as the Silver Horn's attorney, but after marrying Sassy, he'd made the decision to cut down the hours he put in at the ranch and start a practice for himself.

Jett appeared to juggle both jobs without any problems—although Bella didn't know how he kept up with
the workload, especially when he had his own ranch to
deal with, too. But Sassy had taken on a large responsi-
bility of handling the day-to-day running of the J Bar S,
while Noah made sure everything that needed to be
done got done.

"I see you lived through another visit from Mr. Taylor," she said to her brother as she entered his office. "Or
would you like two aspirin and the shades lowered?"

Chuckling, he tossed aside a manila folder and
looked up at her. "If that little man was all I had to
deal with my job would be easy. So what's up with you?
We've not talked all day."

She took a seat in one of the polished wooden chairs
in front of his desk. "I've been busy. And I took on a
case earlier today that has me a bit worried."

Surprise arched his dark brows. "Worried? That's
not like you, sis. You're always confident."

She closed her eyes and massaged the burning lids.
Jett understood that Marcus's infidelity had hurt her
terribly, but no one, not even her brother, realized how
much the experience had trampled her self-worth. Even
now, after acquiring a law degree and proving herself
competent in the courtroom, she still had moments
when she doubted herself. And her effort to get close
to Noah wasn't helping matters. He was the only man
she'd ever tried to pursue and his reluctance to have
anything to do with her was making her feel like a pa-
thetic kitten trying to catch a fierce bald eagle.

Trying to shake the image of Noah from her mind,
she looked at Jett. "Remember Valerie Stanhope? She
was a friend of mine in high school."

"Short girl with mousy brown hair and glasses?"

"That was her. Although the years have turned her into a very pretty woman. Anyway, her brother, Brent, was arrested on theft charges and I agreed to represent him. I've only handled one other criminal case in my life, Jett. What if I bungle this thing and he ends up serving time in prison? I'm not sure I could deal with that on my conscience."

Thoughtful now, he picked up an insulated coffee mug and took a long sip. "What sort of theft? If it's petty, just make a plea deal and forget it. He'll probably be right back in trouble again."

Bella shook her head. "Not petty, thousands. Jewels from the home where he worked as a gardener. Brent swears he never knew about the jewels and Valerie believes the whole thing is a case of insurance fraud."

That caught Jett's attention and he whistled under his breath. "You better have someone do some deep investigating, sis. And that won't be easy or cheap. Did you warn Valerie about the cost?"

"No. I told her not to worry about it. I'll do the digging myself."

Jett groaned. "Oh, Bella, how do you ever expect to make money if you're going to work pro bono?"

"There are more important things to me than padding my bank account."

"Where money is concerned, you've always been more like Dad. It's never ranked very high on your wish list." Shaking his head, he said, "Well, you do only have yourself to support, so I guess it doesn't matter."

Cutting him an annoyed glance, Bella rose from the chair. "Thanks, brother, for reminding me that I'm thirty-two and still have no family."

"Sis, I'm not trying to rub salt in the wound. I happen to believe you're going to find the man of your dreams.

In the meantime, you have a new house. That's something to feel good about."

Her house was beautiful. But without a husband to share the place with, the rooms were nothing more than hollow spaces. She'd give up every square foot, every last stick of furniture if Noah would invite her to live with him in the line-cabin. Did that mean he was the man she wanted to spend the rest of her life with? With each day that passed she was beginning to think so. But was she chasing a fool's dream?

"Yes, my house talks to me every night," she said with bitter humor, then turned to leave the office. "I think I'll call the sheriff's department and see if Evan can give me anything on the Stanhope case."

Jett snorted. "Just because Evan is Sassy's brother doesn't mean he can share department info with you."

Pausing, Bella twisted her head around and frowned at him. "As the guy's lawyer I already have the police report. I want to know what's been written between the lines."

"Good luck. You're going to need it." Jett's mocking chuckles were suddenly interrupted by the telephone. "Just a minute, Bella, it's the ranch calling."

Expecting the caller to be Sassy, who always kept her conversations brief, Bella decided to stick around for another minute, just in case her brother had something better to offer than sarcasm.

After a short moment passed with the phone jammed to his ear, Bella watched his features grow tight. Something was wrong. She could feel it.

"Barbed wire," Jett repeated. "How did that happen?"

Moving back to his desk, she waited anxiously for him to wrap up the call.

After another long stretch of listening, Jett said, "Yeah. Sounds just like Noah. I'll make sure he gets a tetanus shot. Don't worry. You tried and he's stubborn. Thanks for letting me know, honey. I'm closing shop now, so I'll see you in a few minutes."

As Jett hung up the phone, Bella realized her heart was hammering with fear. "Noah has been hurt?"

Although she'd made an effort to keep any note of panic from her voice, the concern she was feeling must have shown on her features because Jett shot her an odd look.

"Sassy tells me the men were mending fence and a piece of barbed wire popped loose of the stretcher. It whacked Noah across the back before finally wrapping around his arm. She says some of the gashes were pretty deep. He refused to go to the doctor, so she stitched up three of the worst wounds and ordered him to go home."

Sassy would be able to do that, Bella thought. The woman was a tough-as-nails ranch hand. She could pull a calf or stitch up a wounded animal as well, or better, than Jett. Still, Noah needed professional medical attention and the urge to race to him was like a storm building inside her.

Telling herself to remain calm, she said, "I thought the guys were moving cattle this week. What were they doing mending fence?"

Jett's eyes narrowed shrewdly. "How did you know the men were moving cattle? You been talking to Sassy?"

Bella quickly turned her gaze to the window and the busy traffic beyond. "Uh—that's right. We talked a couple of nights ago. She must've told me. Or maybe you mentioned it."

Bella actually had spoken with her sister-in-law, but

nothing had been said about cattle or horses. The two women had discussed the children and the celebration Sassy was planning for little Skyler's upcoming birthday. It wasn't that Bella cared if Jett knew about Noah having supper with her a few nights ago. She and her brother had always been very close and they shared their thoughts and feelings about things with each other. But she instinctively knew that Noah wouldn't appreciate her saying anything about their encounters to Jett. Noah was a deeply private man and until he gave her a signal otherwise, she wasn't going to let on to Jett, or anyone, that the two of them had spent time together.

Besides, she thought dismally, five days had passed since Noah had kissed her good-night and she'd not seen or heard from him. Twice she'd heard his truck rumbling by her place as he drove to his cabin, but he'd not stopped either time.

Because he didn't want to get involved with her, she thought glumly. Not on a meaningful level. He seemed to have enjoyed kissing her and if she really tried, she might seduce him into her bed. But that would be as far as he'd let his feelings toward her go. That's why she needed to face facts and move her attention to a man who might really love her.

You'd better go try to find all those dreams with another man.

If she'd use some common sense, she'd follow those cutting words Noah had thrown at her, Bella thought sadly. But the memory of his kiss and the way her heart melted at the mere touch of his fingers were enough to convince her to not give up on the man.

While thoughts of Noah had been churning inside her head, Jett had shut down his computer and was now gathering a slew of papers he'd strung across his desk.

"Well, the hands have been moving cattle, but a fence got torn down in the process and that's where the barbed wire came in." He glanced over at her. "I'm finished here. I'm going to head on home so I can check on Noah. The stubborn mule-head. If I didn't care about the guy so much, I'd kick him in the rear."

"I realize you stay in shape, brother, but you might have a little trouble doing that. Noah's not exactly puny."

Laughing, Jett stuffed a few papers in a briefcase and jammed the worn leather holder beneath his arm. "That's why I'm not going to try it, dear sister." On his way to the door, he pecked a kiss on her cheek. "Are you working late this evening?"

"I have another appointment in thirty minutes. I'll see you tomorrow."

He left through a back entryway and locked the door behind him. Once he was gone, Bella realized her legs were wobbly and she sank into one of the chairs in front of Jett's desk.

Noah had been injured. She'd not expected the news to affect her this much. Especially when it wasn't a life-threatening issue. But it could have been, she thought sickly. If the wire had hit his eye he could have been blinded. Or if it had slashed an artery he could have easily bled to death before reaching a medical facility in town.

A light tapping noise had her looking around to see Peta's face peering around the edge of the door. "Is anything wrong, Bella? I heard Jett leaving and he didn't say a word."

"There was a little accident at the ranch. He's left to make sure everything is okay."

The secretary walked into the room. "Oh, I hope it wasn't serious."

"Don't worry. Everything is under control."

Except her emotions, Bella thought.

Moving closer, Peta carefully scanned Bella's face. "I'm glad to hear that. But are you sure you're okay? You look pale and, well, tense."

Forcing a smile, Bella waved her hand in a dismissive way. "Oh, that's just because I'm dieting. The more I think about not eating, the more it wears on my nerves."

The secretary laughed. "I know the feeling. But Bella, you have a fabulous figure. You don't need to diet."

Rising to her feet, Bella attempted to put a cheery look on her face. "You're too kind, Peta. Now, let's get back to work. The Morrison divorce case is on the court docket tomorrow. I need to make certain my paperwork is in order before I face the judge. Would you get that file for me?"

"I'll have it for you in just a minute."

Bella returned to her office and, as promised, Peta appeared almost instantly with the file in hand. She thanked the secretary and after Peta left the room, Bella opened the file and tried to focus on the legal documents. But all she could see was Noah, his flesh ripped and bleeding.

Everything inside her was screaming to go to him. But Jett was already on his way to Noah's cabin. It would look ridiculous for her to follow. And since Noah had never offered to share his cell phone number with her, she couldn't even call him.

Something between a disgusted groan and a helpless sob slipped past her throat and she dropped her head in her hands. She was either turning into the biggest fool of the century or a woman in love. Either way, Bella had a feeling she was tumbling straight toward a heartache.

* * *

Later that evening, dusk was spreading shadows around the cabin as Noah sat on the front step. Between his legs, Jack rubbed back and forth and emitted a string of coarse meows.

"You're not fooling me, you old codger. This isn't a display of sympathy for my wounds. You want me to get up and get you something else to eat. Like a can of tuna. But that's too bad. I'm all out of tuna."

Instead of meowing another loud protest, Jack went on sudden alert, his unblinking green eyes staring out at the road that dead-ended in front of the cabin.

Knowing the cat could hear sounds he never could, Noah followed Jack's frozen gaze, but saw nothing except a few tufts of grass bending to the breeze.

"There's nothing there, boy. No bear or coyote. But maybe a little field mouse you've been terrorizing has found out where you live and he's come for revenge. Huh?"

The cat moved off the step at the same time Noah heard the faint tinkle of a bell and the crunch of footsteps on gravel.

"What the hell is she doing?" he muttered the question more to himself than the curious cat.

Noah had already risen to his feet, when he spotted Bella rounding a curve in the road. The sight of her caused his stomach to clench, his jaw to tighten. These past few days, he'd purposely avoided stopping at her house. Mainly because he knew that each minute he spent with the woman brought him closer to making love to her.

Moving off the step, he stood on the rough ground and waited for her to get within earshot. Then, not bothering with a greeting, he asked, "What are you doing walking? Is your car on the blink?"

"The road from my house to here is too rough for my little car," she explained. "So I walked."

Since he'd left her house a few nights ago, he'd halfway convinced himself that Bella wasn't really as pretty or sexy as the image he carried in his mind. But he'd only been fooling himself. Just looking at her made him ache with longing.

"You shouldn't have. Dusk is when the predators go on the prowl."

She lifted her wrist to show him she was wearing a bear bell, then quickly slipped it off her wrist and jammed it down in the pocket of her jeans. "It's not even a quarter of a mile from here to my place and I'm the only one prowling about this evening," she said, then gestured toward the yellow tom, who'd sidled up to Noah's leg. "Who's that? I didn't see him the day I was up here."

"Jack isn't always around. He comes and goes whenever he gets the notion."

A smile tilted her lips as she eyed the cat. "He's a handsome guy. I'm surprised he doesn't go back to the barn and stay with his furry friends."

"Jack isn't a barn cat. When he was just a baby, I found him alone on the edge of the highway."

"And you've had him ever since. He's lucky that you rescued him." She bent down to pet the feline, but before she could put a hand on him, Jack quickly dashed off into the shadows. "Well, I can tell he definitely belongs to you."

Noah couldn't help but smile. "I've taught him to be cautious."

"No doubt," she said with a laugh, then her expression grew serious as she gestured toward his bandaged forearm. "I was in Jett's office when Sassy called him about your accident. I wanted to come see for myself how you're doing."

Did she really care that much? The notion tore at him. He couldn't deny he wanted her love and attention. Yet the scarred, cynical part of him didn't want to risk having everything, including his heart, torn away. Enduring that sort of loss once in a man's life was more than enough.

"Well, I can tell you that my arm is stiff and sore and my back ouches if I move a certain way, but otherwise I'm fine. Didn't Jett tell you?"

"I had to work late this evening," she said. "I haven't seen Jett since he left the office to come up here."

He mouthed a curse word under his breath. "Jett shouldn't have bothered on my account. Jack gives me worse scratches than this whenever I try to give him a dose of wormer."

She rolled her eyes. "Jett cares about you. So do I. That's why we bothered to check on you."

Besides the Sundell family, only one other person had ever really cared about Noah and that had been Ward Stevens. Yet even his old partner had eventually turned his back on Noah. But not before he'd sworn to forget the very name of Noah Crawford. Sooner or later, Jett and Bella would do the same. That's what happened with people he let himself get close to.

"Come on," he said gruffly. "I'll make us some coffee."

She followed him into the house and he shut the door against the cooling night air. A lamp was already on in the living area of the small room. Noah walked over to the kitchen and switched on a light above the sink.

"Let me make the coffee," she insisted. "You don't need to be moving your arm. You might tear the cuts open."

He grunted with amusement. "Not hardly. Sassy has me trussed up tighter than a stuffed turkey."

Bella moved over to the short span of cabinets and he stood to one side watching the subtle movements of her body as she gathered the makings for the coffee. Tonight she was wearing black jeans and a thin white blouse tucked inside the waistband. Her dark hair hung loose against her back and swung against the fabric like a curtain pushed and pulled by a gentle breeze.

Unable to ignore the desire rising up in him, he walked up behind her and slipped his good arm around her waist. She dropped the spoon of coffee grounds onto the cabinet and then with a little moan, fell back against him.

Noah bent his head and buried his face in the side of her fragrant hair. "You shouldn't be here," he murmured. "But I'm glad you are, Bella."

She twisted around to look anxiously up at him. "When I heard you'd had an accident it scared me. An incident like that can be deadly." She touched a hand to his cheek. "Are you sure you're okay?"

"What I'm feeling right now is a lot more dangerous than a few cuts on my arm," he said huskily.

"Noah—"

The soft invitation in her eyes was almost his undoing. Before he caved in to temptation, he quickly stepped back and sucked in a deep breath.

"You'd better fix the coffee, Bella."

A look of frustration stole over her face, but she didn't argue or reach to touch him. Instead, she turned back to the cabinet and began cleaning up the spilled coffee grounds.

Moving to the other side of the room where the couch faced the small fireplace, he started to take a seat, then decided he was too restless to sit. Especially with her up and moving about the kitchen.

He ended up standing by the open window, watching the distant mountains being swallowed up by a darkening sky, and wondering why he was such a coward. Why couldn't he simply take what Bella was offering and be thankful she wanted to be near him?

Because she's not just any woman, Noah. She's beautiful, classy and a successful lawyer to boot. She's not the sort to have an empty affair. She's looking for a man to love. A man to be her husband. And she's looking straight at you. That's why you're scared.

Annoyed at the voice in his head, he looked over at Bella. "If you'd like I can turn on the radio or CD player. I have a stack of old standards. Jo Stafford, Dinah Washington, that sort of music. And I have a collection of Western swing and cowboy trail songs."

"That's a strange combination," she said. "I figured you for the modern country stuff—dancing on a barroom floor dusted with sawdust."

He let out a short laugh. "Me, dance? I have two left feet. Besides, that was my father's thing and it triggered many fights with my parents. I think that's why that sort of entertainment never appealed to me."

She said, "Our father spent a lot of time in nightclubs. But he was there to play in a band. Not to drink or pick up women. He wasn't that kind of guy."

She poured water into a fast-drip coffee machine and closed the lid. "But back to your question. I think I could use the quiet tonight, if you don't mind. Peta, our secretary at work, always keeps music going in the background, which is good. It keeps our offices from feeling like tombs. But sometimes it's nice not to hear anything, especially after a hectic day like today."

The weariness in her voice prompted him to return to her side. "I hope you didn't let my little run-in with a piece of barbed wire ruin your day."

Sighing, she shoved a hand through her hair and for the first time tonight Noah noticed her eyes looked tired. The fact struck him hard. For some reason, he'd never imagined Bella putting in an exhausting day of work, or agonizing over her job. The times he'd seen her, she always looked fresh and full of energy. He'd assumed her finances were so secure she could make her workday as light or as busy as she wanted. Apparently her world wasn't that easy.

"I was worried about you," she admitted. "But it all started this morning. I took on a criminal case. That's something I don't normally do. Now I'm afraid I've made a mistake."

"If you feel that uncertain, why did you take the case in the first place?" Two weeks ago, he would've never asked Bella such a question. Before that day he'd stopped to help her with Mary Mae, he hadn't wanted to know what went on in her day-to-day life. He had no desire to hear about her hopes and fears or anything in between. Distance. That was the safe way to treat a provocative woman like Bella. But somehow she'd closed the distance between them and now, damn it, he wanted to know her every thought.

Sighing, she turned back to the coffeepot. As she filled two cups with the steaming brown liquid, she said, "An old friend asked for my help and I couldn't refuse her."

"That's admirable. Helping out a friend."

She handed him one of the coffees and they moved over to the couch. Thinking he'd put as much space as possible between them, Noah sat on one end. But Bella eased onto the middle cushion to leave only inches separating their knees.

After she took a careful sip of coffee, she said, "That's just it. I don't know if I can handle this case. All afternoon I've been wondering if I should tell her to find a more experienced lawyer. You see, this is about her brother. He's been arrested on theft charges. And from what she tells me it sounds like a frame job."

Noah felt like cold water had been thrown straight at his face. He knew exactly what it meant to be set up for a fall. He'd not forgotten how the lies and suspicions had eaten at his insides until there'd been nothing left but the shell of a man.

He stared blindly at the floor as his past rushed at him from all directions. "What about the brother?" he asked stiffly. "What's his story?"

"I've not talked to him yet. I'm planning to do that tomorrow. Along with a request to get his bail lowered."

He sipped his coffee in hopes the warm, rich brew would ease the frozen muscles in his throat. "So you think he deserves a chance to tell his side of things?"

Noah could feel her brown gaze boring into the side of his face and from the corner of his eye he could see the space between her brows pucker with confusion. "Well, naturally. Why wouldn't he deserve a chance? Everyone should be considered innocent until proven guilty."

"That's only in a fairy-tale world, Bella. In real life things don't work that way."

"You say that like—have you ever been in trouble with the law?"

He cut her a skeptical glance. "And if I said yes, would that make you get up and leave?"

"No. Everyone makes mistakes of one kind or another. If you have, I figure you've already paid for them."

"I've paid for them all right," he said cynically. "But if it will ease your mind I've never had any run-ins with the law."

She placed her cup on a small table where he kept a stack of reading material, then scooted across the cushion until her thigh was pressed alongside his. Noah watched with a mixture of fear and fascination as she brought her hands up to frame his face.

"Noah," she said softly, "there's so much about you that I don't know or understand. I wish you'd share your thoughts with me. Even a little would make me happy."

The gentle way her hands were cradling his cheeks was unlike anything he'd experienced before. The affection flowing from her fingertips left him feeling cornered and vulnerable and far too weak to pull away.

"You're asking a lot from me, Bella." His voice sounded oddly thick, as though he'd just woken from a deep sleep.

An enticing little smile curved her lips as she murmured, "That's because I want to give you a lot."

Her mouth moved toward his and Noah couldn't deny her or the need inside him. He closed the fraction of distance between their lips and the sweet taste of her instantly flooded his senses, and sent desire throbbing through his body.

He started to draw her closer, then realized he was still holding onto his coffee. Without breaking the contact of their lips, he somehow managed to lower the cup over the arm of the couch and set it safely on the floor. Once he was rid of the hindrance, he wrapped his arms around her and pulled her upper body onto his.

Her breasts flattened against his chest, while her mouth parted, inviting him to take more. Desire shot straight to his brain and sent a torrential rain of heat pouring through his body.

Like a starved man, his tongue thrust past her lips and began a slow, seductive exploration of the ribbed roof of her mouth, the sharp edges of her teeth. Immediately her tongue tangled with his, causing an erotic dance to ensue and all the while he could hear her soft whimpers, feel her fingers digging into his upper shoulders.

The urgency of her kiss drove him onward and he couldn't touch her enough, kiss her enough. As his lips feasted on hers, his hands roamed her shoulders and back before finally slipping low enough to cup around her bottom.

Bella was the first to finally tear her mouth away and as she sucked in long, raspy breaths, she pulled apart the snaps on his shirt.

Once the fabric fell away to expose his bare skin, she said, "I wondered if the rest of you was as brown as your face. Now I can see for myself that you are."

Helpless with need, Noah couldn't do anything to stop the reckless path they were taking. And when she lowered her head and touched her tongue to the center of his chest, his last exhausted attempt to resist collapsed. Like a dam trying to hold back churning flood waters, it burst wide and suddenly it was far too late to push her aside and walk away from the danger.

Slowly, the tip of her tongue made a swathe of moist

circles upon his skin until the throbbing need inside him built to an unbearable pressure. Finally, he thrust his hands in her hair and gently lifted her head. And when his gaze connected with her smoky brown gaze, he was too overwhelmed to speak.

"Am I hurting your arm? Your back?" she whispered.

"You're making me hurt all right. But not in those places," he told her in a voice rough with desire.

The corners of her lips tilted upward as she slipped her warm hands down over his rib cage and farther downward to the button on the waistband of his jeans.

"I don't have nursing skills," she said impishly, "but I can try to ease the pain."

He quickly moved them to a sitting position, but even then, she kept her hands on him, as though she feared he still might try to slip away from her grasp. The idea that he could make an escape now was laughable. Except that there was nothing funny about surrendering to this woman's arms. Mistake or not, he was tired of always denying himself the pleasures a man dreamed about, the love he needed to make himself whole.

"Bella." He breathed her name as he nuzzled his nose against her cheek. "I don't want this to happen and then you have regrets."

She eased her head back far enough to look into his eyes and in that moment Noah felt like a very young man, one who'd never been intimate with a woman before. Just touching Bella, looking into her eyes and having her hands move over him felt different and new. And so wonderful it nearly sucked his breath away.

"I don't want you to have regrets either, Noah. That would hurt me more than anything."

"Bella, I—

Before he could finish, she gently placed a finger

upon his lips. "You don't have to say it. Neither of us can predict the future. You've already told me no promises. I can live with that for now."

She could live with it at this very moment, Noah thought, but how would she feel later? How long would it be before she wanted more from him? Things that he could never give her? Like marriage, a home and children?

He wasn't going to dwell on those questions tonight, Noah decided. No, for now he was going to simply enjoy the fact that a beautiful woman wanted to be in his bed. Tomorrow would be soon enough to deal with the consequences.

Chapter Seven

Noah rose from the couch and pulled her along with him. Once she was standing beside him, Bella's legs began to tremble as if she'd just jogged a fast five miles.

With a breathless little laugh, she snatched a hold on his arm to steady herself. "I think you've knocked my legs out from under me, cowboy."

"I can fix that." Bending forward, he put an arm around her back and the other beneath her legs, then lifted her easily off the floor. "Just hang on."

"Noah! Your arm—the cuts!"

"Shh. A little flyweight like you isn't going to hurt my arm."

Past the tiny kitchen, a door led into a shadowy bedroom. As he carried her into the small space, she caught a glimpse of a standard-sized bed with an iron slatted head and footboard and covered with a light-colored patchwork quilt. Along the outside wall, a window stood open, allowing the pine-scented breeze to drift into the quiet haven.

At the side of the mattress, Noah set her down on a braided rug, but kept his arms planted firmly around her. Their strength and warmth enveloped her with a sense of homecoming and she wondered if he had any clue as to how much he was affecting her. How much he was coming to mean to her.

Her heart was thumping wildly and the more she breathed, the more light-headed she felt. It seemed as if she'd wanted to make love to Noah forever. From the first moment she'd ever laid eyes on him, a feeling of wild, wicked desire had popped into her mind. It hadn't made sense then. But it did now. And as she slipped her arms around him, she felt as though her life was just beginning.

Tilting her head back, she met his gaze and a swell of emotions caused tears to sting her eyes. "Noah, it's been a long time since I—well, have been with a man. Please forgive me if I'm awkward."

His hands gently cradled the back of her head. "Oh, Bella. You could never be anything but perfect. And anyway, I'm not exactly Mr. Romeo."

She splayed her hands against his bare chest and curled her fingers into the patch of curly black hair. "You are to me, Noah," she whispered. "And I want you just as you are."

"You don't know what you're saying. But right now I don't care. All I care about is you. And this."

His head dipped to hers and then his lips were on hers, creating a magic that caused her head to buzz. Excitement hummed along her veins and the glow deep within her ignited into a scorching flame that took away

her breath and her ability to think. All she could do was
react to the urgings of her body.

Tearing her lips from his, she began to shove his
shirt down over his shoulders. In her haste, she forgot
about the bandages on his forearm, until he winced and
jerked his arm free of the sleeve.

"Oh, Noah, I'm sorry!"

"Forget it." He tossed the denim shirt to the floor.
"Just let me do it. It'll be faster."

She stood to one side, watching as he stripped out
of his jeans, then sat on the edge of the bed to remove
his boots. Once he was down to nothing but a pair of
plain white boxers, he reached out and pulled her between his legs. But not before she'd caught an eyeful
of broad shoulders and a wide chest dusted with curly
black hair. A corded abdomen narrowed down to a trim
waist, while the long legs pressed on either side of her
were all hard, sinewy muscle.

Being this close to his naked body, with the masculine scent of his bare skin wafting all around her was
all it took to send ripples of excitement rushing through
her. When his fingers began to clumsily deal with the
buttons on her shirt, her nipples tightened with antici-
pation, her body ached to be connected to his.

Curving her hands over both of his shoulders, she
leaned closer, while mentally willing his hands to move
faster.

"I thought you said you could do this faster," she said
in a breathless rush.

He groaned with frustration. "I thought I could. But
these damned buttons are too little for my big fingers."

"Let me do it this way." Brushing his hands aside,
she grabbed the hem of the shirt and quickly tugged it
over her head.

After she'd tossed the garment to the heap of clothing he'd already made on the floor, he stood and lifted her onto the bed.

"Be still," he ordered as he reached for the closure on her jeans. "I can handle a pair of jeans."

While he dealt with the button and zipper, Bella focused on the black waves of hair falling over his forehead. She'd never been this close to such a rugged, sexy man and the idea of making love to him was more potent than a shot of whiskey.

By the time he'd stripped her down to nothing but a set of pale pink lacy underwear and joined her on the bed, she was trembling with need, her breaths coming and going in jerky spurts.

He rolled her toward him and she wrapped her arms around his neck and aligned the front of her body next to his. With one arm, he pressed even closer and the sensation of his heated skin sliding against her breasts caused a shiver to ripple through her and a moan to find its way past her lips.

"You feel like a piece of hot satin against me."

His voice was rough with desire and the sound was just as provocative as the touch of his hands moving against her back and down to the lace covering her hips.

"And you feel like everything I've ever wanted," she whispered. "Make love to me, Noah."

He tilted her chin to an angle where his lips could reach hers. His kiss swallowed up her sigh and then he broke the contact between their lips to begin a slow, sweet caress along the side of her throat.

Eventually the tempting kisses reached her collarbone and his hand found its way to the middle of her back to unfasten her bra. Once the flimsy garment slipped away from her breasts, his hands cupped their fullness while his gaze devoured the plump flesh.

When his head lowered and he drew a puckered nipple into his mouth, she cried out with pleasure and thrust her hands into his thick hair. His tongue laved the sensitive bud until she was writhing against him, desperate for even the tiniest form of relief.

Eventually, the hot throbbing in her nipple spread downward until it pooled in the intimate spot between her thighs. The unbearable ache caused her to tug on his hair and lift his head away from her breast.

"Noah—I—can't—wait! I need to feel you inside me! Now!"

Her frantic urgings pushed Noah's desire to the boiling point and it was all he could do to stay in control as he peeled off his shorts and rolled her onto her back.

Once he'd positioned himself over her, he took a moment to look down and as he gazed at her partially closed eyes and swollen lips, her dark hair lying in tangled strands upon the worn quilt, he was quite certain he'd never seen anything more lovely or precious.

"Bella. Oh, Bella, I wanted this to be slow and sure and perfect. But I—"

He didn't finish the rest as she suddenly snatched a hold on his hips and jerked him downward.

"It will be all those things next time," she whispered.

With her hand on his manhood, she guided him into her soft, warm folds. After that Noah wasn't aware of anything except the movement of her body rising up to his, her hands skimming over his back and buttocks, the hot trail of her lips against his skin and the feel of her teeth sinking gently into his shoulder.

The need she was building in him far outweighed

anything he'd ever felt before and the realization rocked the ground beneath him. As he frantically drove himself into her, flashes of the room spun wildly around him, while outside the window, the sound of calling night birds faintly registered through the hazy fog.

Tiny particles in his brain were questioning whether he'd gone crazy. If he had, then crazy was a place he didn't want to leave. For the first time in his life he wanted to give the deepest part of himself to a woman, and the feeling was so euphoric he wondered if he must be dying. No living man could feel like this and still be alive.

Time ceased to matter as over and over their bodies crashed together in a perfect rhythm that grew faster and faster until Noah's breath was gone and his heart pounded as if something wild had suddenly inhabited his chest.

Beneath him, Bella was groaning, her hands gripping his buttocks. And then suddenly she was arching and straining against him.

"Noah. My Noah!"

She was slipping over the edge and taking him with her. The frantic fall had him snatching her upper body close to his and with his mouth on hers, he made one final thrust. The release was so great he was certain he'd been catapulted to heaven. Every cell in his body felt like a glowing star and for one brief instant he felt immense happiness.

Rolling away from her, he lay on his back and fixed his gaze on the open window. His breathing was still coming in rapid gulps and though his heartbeat had slowed, it continued to throb loudly in his ears.

He'd never felt more weak and vulnerable in his life. Yet there was a sense of contentment in him that contradicted each doubt that swirled through his mind. In the end, he didn't know which feeling would win out, but for the moment it didn't matter. All that mattered was the fact that Bella was lying next to him. His bed was no longer empty. And neither was his heart.

Sighing, she turned onto her side so that she was facing him. Noah looked over at her and winced with longing as he scanned the soft light in her eyes and the tender smile curving her lips.

"I don't know what to say, Noah. Except that nothing like this has ever happened to me. Not like this."

Her hand reached over and came to rest in the middle of his chest. Noah lifted it to his lips and kissed the tips of her fingers.

"It shouldn't have happened here in this old cabin. You deserve much better."

She scooted close enough to press a kiss against his damp shoulder. "This old cabin, as you call it, was built by my grandfather. I happen to like it. Besides, what just happened between us would have been just as great if we'd been on the ground underneath a pine tree."

The fact that she looked at everything so simply and logically made it impossible for Noah to express his feelings. She couldn't understand his thoughts or fears. He'd be wasting his time to try to explain them.

"Yeah. I expect it would," was all he could manage to say.

Propping herself up on one elbow, she gave him a long, pointed look. "I told you I would have no regrets, Noah. And I don't. But I'm not so sure you can say the same for yourself."

With a groan of frustration, he pulled her head down to his and cupped his hand against her damp cheek. "If you're thinking I regret what just happened, you're wrong. I feel blessed and honored to have you here with me."

Her soft brown eyes swept over his face. "And what about happy? That's how I want you to be, Noah. Happy."

He tried to smile and the effort made him realize the expression was one he'd rarely displayed in his lifetime. "I'm not sure I know what that is, Bella. If I was ever happy, the feeling didn't stick around. Maybe because I'm not capable of holding on to it. Or maybe I just didn't know what it was when I had it. Either way, you don't need to be worrying yourself about pleasing me. You've given me more than I ever expected to have."

Her hand moved gently over his chest and Noah wondered if this might be how it felt to be touched by an angel. Bella was making him feel wanted and needed and that was a heavenly thing.

The need to put an end to his soft thoughts made him ease away from her and rise from the bed. After fishing his shorts from the pile of clothing, he tugged them on and walked over to the window.

As he breathed in the cool night air, he hoped the sharp, tangy scent of the pines would help to clear his mind. Yet he knew that nothing on earth would be able to erase the passion he'd just experienced with Bella.

So what was he going to do now? How would he be able to keep his hands off her? And if he couldn't, what would it do to his job, his friendship with Jett? He'd worked so hard to start his life over here on the J Bar S. If everything ended, he wasn't sure he'd have the will to start over again.

The deep thoughts were churning around in his head when Bella came to stand next to him.

"The night is beautiful," she said quietly. "The crescent moon looks like it's pouring silver dust over the mountains."

"It would be prettier if a band of clouds were pouring rain."

She chuckled. "Spoken like a true Nevada rancher," she said, then looked up at him. "Tell me how you came to be a cowboy and rancher, Noah. Was it something you always wanted to do?"

Noah had never talked much about his past. Sometimes with the ranch hands, he'd bring up a story or two about an ornery horse he'd ridden, or a particularly bad spell of weather he'd worked in. But that was as far as his reminiscing went. Bella deserved more than that, though.

"When I was just a little kid, I'd see cowboys on television and a few around the small town where we lived. But all I knew about them was that they rode horses and chased cows."

A knowing smile tilted her lips. "And that seemed exciting to you."

"Well, not any more than a fireman or policeman or some job like that." He slanted her a wry glance. "My parents weren't exactly the sort to encourage education. Being a lawyer like you was as far out of reach as becoming president of the United States."

"In other words, your parents never asked you if you wanted to be a doctor or lawyer."

He let out a caustic laugh. "Hell, my parents couldn't even figure out where their own lives were going. They weren't concerned about what their little snot-nosed boy might grow up to be."

Her hand rested on his arm. "I wish—well, that things had been different—better for you."

He shook his head. "I'm not telling you this for sympathy, Bella. I made out okay. I had a roof over my head and food to eat. And when I went to live with my grandparents some things got better. They had a fairly nice house, plenty to eat, and the utilities were never turned off. But Granddad was a rigid, narrow-minded man, who believed everyone should see things his way. Even if I'd wanted to go to college, he wouldn't have helped. For one thing he was a miser. Secondly, he was a retired copper miner. The job had made him a decent living and he thought I was stupid for not wanting to do the same."

Shivering slightly, she hugged her arms to her chest. "So what happened? How did you go from your grandfather demanding you become a miner, to working as a cowboy?"

Noah shut the window, then took her by the shoulder. "You're cold. Let's go back to bed."

Once they were under the covers and Bella's head was pillowed on his shoulder, he asked, "Warm now?"

"Mmm. Just right." She hugged her arm around his chest. "Now finish telling me about your grandfather."

She wasn't going to let the story of his young life die. Not until he'd finished the whole thing. But oddly enough, now that Noah had started talking, it was far easier than he'd expected.

"There's not a whole lot more to tell, Bella. I learned early on that it was useless to argue my point. So I kept quiet and stayed out of his way as much as I could. When I was fourteen a friend found us a job on a nearby ranch mucking out horse stalls. We were too young to drive, so every day we had to walk five miles out from town and back. But we didn't mind. I fell in love with the livestock and the land and decided I wanted to become a rancher. The foreman was a nice guy and could see I wanted to learn. He and the hands took me under their wings, taught me how to rope and ride and deal with livestock."

"So how long did you work there?"

"For the next four summers. That was long enough to learn about the work involved in keeping a ranch going."

"From living on the J Bar S, I've learned it's never-ending work," she replied, then asked, "How did your grandfather feel about all this? Was he proud you were learning a trade?"

He snorted. "Proud? Oh, Bella. He didn't see me as a grandson. He saw me as a nuisance. As soon as I turned eighteen and graduated high school, I went off on my own and I've been taking care of myself ever since."

"Did you ever go back to visit your grandparents?"

He sighed. "I've gone back to Benson once and that was to attend my grandmother's funeral. She'd been a good woman and deserved more than what she'd gotten from her husband. Then three years later I learned Granddad had died. But by the time I'd heard about him passing, he'd already been buried. Which was just as well. I don't think I would have gone to say good-bye to him."

When several moments passed and she didn't say anything Noah decided he'd finally managed to break through to her. The account of his childhood had suc-ceeded in bursting the fairy-tale bubble she'd built around him. They weren't from the same stock. In a few minutes she'd find some excuse to get dressed and make a beeline back to her fancy house. He should be feeling relief; instead he felt dead inside.

Finally, she said, "When you first told me how your father dumped you onto your grandparents, I wondered how a man could do such a thing. How he could turn out to be such a callous and, frankly, worthless human being? But it's easy to understand now. He didn't know how to love you or be a father. How could he? He'd never had a loving father to teach him."

"I didn't have one, either, Bella. It's a defect in my family that's been passed on and on. That's why it has to stop with me. That's why I'm not about to father a child or take a wife."

She lifted her head to look at him. "Cycles can be broken, Noah. And you're strong enough to break it. That is, if you want to."

Did he want to break the cycle and be everything his father and grandfather hadn't been? There'd been plenty of times Noah had watched Jett interacting with his children and he'd wondered how it would be to have a little person of his own to look to him for love and guidance and security. To have a part of him live on through his children was something most every man wanted. But Noah could see that being a father was a job that was far too complex for him to handle. Still, the idea that she believed in him, even after all that he'd revealed about himself, was enough to warm his heart.

Beneath the covers his hand slipped up and down her arm. "This guy you're going to defend. I'm glad you're taking his case."

Her head stirred against his shoulder and he knew she was studying his face in the darkness.

"You are? Why?"

"Because sometimes a guy just needs someone to believe in him."

Shifting so that her upper body was lying across his chest, she brought her lips next to his. "We all need that, my dear Noah."

Like a soppy fool, emotions filled his throat and

made it impossible to speak. But Noah figured he'd already said more than enough tonight.

With a groan of fresh desire, he deepened the kiss
and when her arms fastened tightly around him, he
pushed everything from his mind, except making love
to Bella.

On Thursday of the following week, on her way
home from work, Bella stopped by Jett and Sassy's to
spend a few minutes with her nephews and niece.

When she entered the house, she found Sassy in the
kitchen dicing vegetables and cutting strips of beef to
make fajitas. Skyler, her three-year-old daughter, was
sitting on the floor with a coloring book and a small
box of crayons. The girl was dressed in jeans and boots,
while the flowered headband holding back her straw-
berry curls gave her a sweet, girly look.

The minute she spotted Bella entering the room, she
raced over and hugged her little arms tightly around
her legs.

"Auntie Bella! Look, Mommy! Auntie Bella is here!"

The tall woman with a thick red French braid hanging against her back, turned away from her task at the
cabinet to greet Bella.

"Well, hello, stranger," she said with a wide smile.
"I was beginning to wonder if you'd disowned us or
something. You haven't stopped by in days."

Bella reached down and lifted Skyler into her arms,
then cuddling the girl close to her, she walked over to
Sassy.

"I've been extra busy this week," she told her sister-
in-law.

"Jett tells me the office is getting busier and busier."

Work wasn't the only thing that had kept Bella busy

this past week. Each evening she'd been racing home, hoping that Noah would stop by to spend time with her.

The night she'd spent with Noah at his cabin had been magical and the next morning she'd emerged into a different world. Everything around her had seemed bright and vividly alive. Each minute of every day was special because it brought her that much closer to being in Noah's arms again.

Crazy or not, she'd given more to him that night than just her body. She'd given him her heart and everything that went with it. Her hopes and dreams and plans were all wrapped up in one tall, rugged rancher—even though she still had no idea what he was really thinking about her or the future.

Since then he had relented and stayed one night at her house. On another occasion, he'd eaten supper with her, but before the evening had progressed to the bedroom, he'd been called away on an emergency with a downed fence and loose cattle. That was three nights ago and she'd not heard from him since. The time apart was not only making her ache to see him, it was also making her wonder if something had caused him to change his mind about her and the two of them being together.

"Very busy. Peta doesn't want help, but we're going to have to hire another secretary soon. Are you sure you don't want the job?" Bella asked teasingly.

Sassy laughed. "Oh sure, why not? Between being a wife, mother, cook, housekeeper and ranch hand, I might as well add secretary."

Bella chuckled. "I know I've said this a thousand times, Sassy, but you're incredible. Jett is a lucky man."

A look of deep affection came over Sassy's lovely face. "No. You got it wrong, Bella. I'm the lucky one to have Jett."

"And Gypsy, don't forget her," Bella tacked on. Gypsy was a young Shoshone woman who worked during the day as the children's nanny. At night she went home to live with her grandparents in nearby Silver City.

"Yes, thank God for Gypsy," Sassy replied. "I couldn't do half of what I do without her help. I just hope she waits a few years before she finds a man and starts having babies of her own."

"Auntie Bella, we have a new baby!"

Skyler's announcement had her glancing down at the child, then tossing a questioning look at Sassy.

She let out a hearty laugh. "No. She doesn't mean that. Not yet."

"Yet? So you and Jett are thinking about another baby soon?"

"Why stop at three?"

Why indeed, Bella thought. Her brother and sister-in-law were deeply in love and they cherished their children. At one time, Bella had expected to have her own family by this stage of her life. But a cheating husband and a bitter divorce had gotten in the way.

Before Bella could give Sassy a reply, Skyler's little hand was patting her cheek in an attempt to get her attention.

"The new baby has spots on his rump. And his legs go like this." She made a wobbly gesture with her arms. "Mommy says he has to learn how to walk. Just like Mason."

"Mason isn't walking now, is he?" Bella asked with dismay. "He's not old enough to pull that off."

Smiling, Sassy turned back to her cutting board. "Skyler thinks her little brother is Superman. She believes Mason should be able to walk at seven months old. The baby she's talking about is our new colt. One of the mustang mares I got from Finn delivered her baby yesterday."

"You wanna see him, Auntie Bella? He's pretty! And he's gonna be mine. Not J.J.'s!"

Laughing at Skyler's emphatic statement, she kissed her niece on the cheek and sat her back on the floor. "I'll have to look at this new baby when I have more time. I have to be heading home soon. By the way, where are your brothers?"

"Daddy took J.J. to the barn," she answered in a sulky tone. "'Cause he's big. I'm big, too, see?"

Bella hid a smile as she watched her niece attempt to make a muscle in her arm.

Sassy groaned. "See," she said to Bella. "Our daughter needs a little sister to have tea parties with and play dolls."

"I don't wanna play with dolls," Skyler argued. "I wanna play with the calves and the new baby horse."

Bella laughed while Sassy shook her head with amused surrender.

"You go finish your coloring," she said to Skyler, "and let me and Auntie Bella finish our talk."

When the child finally made a move to do her mother's bidding, Sassy leveled a pointed look at Bella. "So tell me what's been going on," Sassy urged. "Anything new?"

Only that I've fallen in love with the man I want to spend the rest of my life with. But he doesn't want to make anything permanent with me. That's all, Bella silently answered her question. Aloud she said, "I've taken on a criminal case."

"Yes, Jett mentioned that to me. I think he's a little concerned that you're stressing yourself over the case."

She was stressing herself over Noah, but she couldn't

tell Sassy such a thing. Her relationship with Noah was still something private between just the two of them.

Grimacing, Bella asked, "So my brother thinks I'm not experienced enough to handle it?"

"He didn't say that at all. He only said there's a lot of footwork and digging that goes with criminal cases. That's all."

Bella sighed. "Sorry. I didn't mean to sound defensive. It's just that I've been trying all week to gather useful information that might prove my client's innocence. But so far I've not gotten a break. This afternoon, I met with his accuser and that didn't go well." Pausing, she shook her head. "Actually the woman isn't the accuser, even though it was her jewelry that turned up missing. Her husband is the one who filed the charges."

"You say it didn't go well. What happened? She wouldn't talk?"

"Frankly, something has the woman terrified and I believe it's her husband. Though she didn't tell me that outright. Anyway, I have to find a way to make her open up. Because I'm quite certain she knows far more than she's admitting."

"Well, good luck there." Glancing over her shoulder, she gave Bella a clever smile. "What about your love life? Met anyone new?"

Noah had been here on the J Bar S for more years than Bella. But it wasn't until a few weeks ago that she'd been handed the opportunity to say more than five words to him, see him without anyone else around to distract either one of them. No, he could hardly be considered a newcomer here, she thought, but everything she felt for the man was certainly fresh and new.

"No. Not exactly."

Sassy whirled around, her expression eager. "Not

exactly? Does that mean you've found someone you're getting interested in? Finally?"

Bella tiredly pushed a hand through her tumbled hair. "I guess you could say that."

"Oh! Who is he? Do I know him?"

You see him every day in the ranch yard, Bella wanted to say. Instead, she merely gave her sister-in-law a faint smile. "It's too early to talk about right now, Sassy."

Clearly disappointed, Sassy asked, "Why? Is he married and trying to get a divorce or something?"

"No. Nothing like that. He's just not ready for a relationship."

"Oh, I see." Groaning, Sassy rolled her eyes. "A man finally comes along and turns your head, but he has cold feet. Maybe you ought to look elsewhere, Bella. If you have to drag a man to the altar, he's not worth having."

Even Casper wouldn't be strong enough to pull Noah anywhere near a marriage altar, Bella thought ruefully. But it was too late for her to look at another man. Noah had already taken up a permanent position in her heart.

"You're right, Sassy. If you have to pull love out of a man like a tooth or a splinter, then you're not getting the real thing," she said, then desperately needing to change the subject, she asked, "Is Mason asleep? I'd like to peek in on him before I go."

"Gypsy took him to the nursery more than an hour ago to rock him to sleep. Another tooth is trying to come in so he's been fussy." She motioned Bella out of the kitchen. "Go check on them. It's time he woke up anyway. Otherwise, he'll keep his parents awake all night."

Bella laughed. "Good reason for me to go fetch him."

A half hour later, as Bella drove away from the main

house, Sassy's questions continued to nag at her. Her sister-in-law had wanted to know if the man who'd caught Bella's eye was married or in the process of getting a divorce. Well, Noah wasn't married. That much was evident. But what did Bella really know about Noah's past? Had he ever been in love or engaged? Maybe he'd tried marriage before and it hadn't worked? That could be the reason he was so against the idea of becoming a husband or father.

Other than what he'd told her that night at the cabin about his childhood, he'd said next to nothing about his past. She understood that he wanted to forget the way his family had treated him. But what about the ten years after he'd left Benson and come here to the J Bar S? A lot could happen to a person in that length of time.

Short of robbery or murder, nothing about Noah's past would change the deep feelings she had for him. But something must have happened during those years. Something so heartbreaking it had made him retreat from any desire for love and family. And until she knew what it was, there was no hope in the two of them ever having a future together.

Chapter Eight

Sex. That's all he wanted from Bella. That's all he needed.

For the past several days Noah had been repeating the mantra over and over to himself. But try as he might, he couldn't quite convince himself that the only thing he felt for Bella was physical. Maybe that had something to do with the way his heart swelled every time he thought of her tender smile, the sparkle in her eyes when she looked at him. She was a beautiful angel who believed in him. That was enough to make him love her.

Love? Oh, Lord, no! He didn't love Bella. He wasn't ever going to love anyone again. And nothing she could say or do could change his mind about that.

So what are you going to do, Noah? Just continue to use her because she's so willing and intent on having a relationship with you? What kind of man would that make you? A user like your father and grandfather? If

you were any kind of man at all, you'll end things with
her. You'll set her free to find a loving husband and a
good father for the children she wants.

The accusing voice in his head continued to haunt
him as he drove away from the ranch yard and headed
east toward Bella's house. But the moment he turned
onto her drive and spotted her walking toward the barn,
the hopeless thoughts flew out of his mind. Sooner or
later, he would have to end this insanity. But for right
now, he couldn't ignore this ache he had to be near her.

She must have heard the approach of his truck because she turned and glanced toward the road. The moment she spotted him, she waved and started walking
in his direction.

Noah parked the truck and quickly strode down the
shady path toward the barn. When he got within reach,
she didn't say a word. Instead, she wrapped her arms
around his waist and held on tight for long, long moments.

"My, my. I feel like a lost teddy bear that's just been
found."

Laughing softly, she tilted her head back and smiled
up at him. "I thought you were lost for good. It's been
three days since I've seen you."

Because of his work, Noah was forced to carry a cell
phone. And he used it when necessary. Especially when
he needed to speak with Jett about a ranching matter.
Otherwise, he didn't send text messages or talk on the
phone and he'd warned Bella of the fact when she'd
given him her phone number a few days ago.

"I guess you're thinking I should've taken the time
to call," he said ruefully.

"It would have been nice," she agreed, her smile
forgiving. "But now that you're here it doesn't matter."

"These past few days I've had to work late for one reason or another," he explained. "I thought I was going to get to see you last night, but one of the horses got colic. I ended up staying over on the Horn until two o'clock this morning while Doc Simmons treated him."

"Oh no! Is he going to be okay?"

He shot her a wry grin. "Yeah. And in case you're interested, so am I."

Chuckling, she took him by the hand and urged him toward the barn. "I'm glad to hear you're going to survive, too. You can help me feed the horses. And then if you talk to me nicely, I might feed you, too."

He slanted her a clever look. "I'll try to think up a few sweet words. I'm hungry."

The sight of her smile warmed him as much as the feel of her small hand wrapped firmly around his. By the time they carried the feed out to the horses' trough and returned to the barn to put away the buckets, Noah couldn't keep his hands off her.

In the cool, dim interior of the feed room, he gathered her into his arms.

"I've been dying to do this." He kissed her. "And this," he added, his hands cupping around her breasts.

She dotted rapid-fire kisses on his lips and face, while her hands tugged the tails of his shirt out of his jeans. Her urgent response fed the desire that was already consuming him and he wondered how he could get them both back to the house before he lost all control.

"I've missed you so much, Noah. Make love to me. Now!"

He lifted his head, his gaze desperately searching her face. "Here?"

"Why not?"

The eagerness in her husky voice turned him inside out and before he recognized what was happening, their lips were locked together and he was easing her blouse off her shoulders.

Once the garment fell to the floor, he dropped his head and tasted the creamy skin. "Someone might come down here looking for you."

Her hands shoved at his shirt until her palms were sliding against his bare torso. Three days without her had seemed like an eternity and now that she was touching him, he was certain her fingers had turned to flames, scorching his skin and making him ache for relief.

"They'd call first. No one but you shows up unannounced," she said, her low, husky voice full of amusement.

His lips tracked a moist trail up the side of her neck and along her jawbone. "Want me to stop and give you a call first?"

"You devil. You're not stopping—anything," she finished with a needy groan.

His mouth returned to hers and while they kissed, she guided him backward until they were deep into the room and his legs bumped into a stack of hay bales.

Recognizing her intentions, he allowed her to push him down upon the shelf of hay. With his upper body resting on the makeshift bed and his feet planted firmly on the floor, the pungent scent of alfalfa filled his head. But the smell or the hard stems poking into his back was hardly a detraction from Bella.

Helpless with need, he watched her strip out of her clothing, then waited, his teeth gritted while she opened his fly and freed his throbbing manhood. To have her touching him there was almost too much to bear.

Intent on pulling her beneath him and driving himself into her, Noah jerked upward. But she had other ideas. She shoved him back down and pinned his shoulders against the hay.

"You just lie back and let me do this, cowboy."

Two weeks ago, her boldness would've shocked him. But not now. The few times they'd been together had been enough for familiarity between them to grow. In the beginning he'd fought hard to prevent the closeness from happening. But he'd failed miserably. Now making love to her was as natural as breathing.

"Bella."

Her name was the only word he managed to utter before she moved astride him, then quickly enveloped him into her welcoming body.

The pleasure was so intense he felt sure the hair on his head lifted from his scalp. From his waist down he was on fire and the need to douse it had him grabbing her hips and yanking her downward until their bodies were completely locked together.

"If you're trying to torture me you're succeeding," he said in a choked voice.

"I'm trying to love you," she whispered, then bent her head downward until she could press her lips to his chest. "That's what I want. What I need."

There was something very possessive in her voice. It warned Noah that she had no plans of letting him go now, or in the future. But at the moment he wasn't concerned about the grip she had on him. He'd worry about escaping a heartache later, when his mind was clear and she wasn't using her hands and lips and body to intoxicate him.

What started out fast and frantic ended the same way, but much later, after they'd eaten dinner and retired to Bella's bedroom, they made love again. This time with slow, meticulous pleasure. Once it was over, Noah found it difficult to set his world back on its axis.

Lying on his back, he stared into the darkness and wondered how much longer he could allow this thing with him and Bella to go on. He was falling deeper and deeper into a helpless pit of need. If he didn't climb his way out soon, he doubted he'd ever find the strength. And then what? Just lie back and watch himself ruin Bella's life? And his own?

A long stretch of silence passed before Bella rolled toward him and rested a hand on his arm.

"Are you asleep?"

"No. I thought you were," he answered.

"Mmm. My time with you is too precious to waste sleeping."

His throat thickened, making his voice gruff. "One of these days you're going to look back and wonder why you wasted all this time on me."

Sighing, she scooted off the opposite side of the bed and Noah watched her pull on an emerald-green robe and patter barefoot over to a set of French doors. Once she'd opened them wide and the cool night breeze was wafting into the room, she returned to the bed and sat down on the edge of the mattress.

"So you think I won't always want you here with me?" she asked.

Releasing a heavy breath, he shifted onto his side so that he could see her. Now that she'd opened the doors, silvery moonlight was illuminating the room and bathing her profile with a soft glow. Never in his life had he ever dreamed he'd be this close to a woman like her.

"I know you won't," he answered.

"Why not?"

"Because pretty soon the sex will cool and then I won't have anything to offer you."

"That kind of talk is insulting to both of us."

"Sorry, Bella. I'm a realist. Not a romantic." He gestured to their surroundings. "Look at this room and compare it to my bedroom in the cabin."

Shaking her head, she traced her fingers alongside his cheek. "That room will always be special to me. Because it was where we first made love."

No, where we first had sex, he wanted to correct her. But he couldn't. In her mind it was love and he didn't want to hurt her any more than he had to.

"Besides," she went on, "what does this damned room have anything to do with us?"

He groaned. "Bella, I'm not a pauper. I have money saved and a small herd of cattle to build on. But I could never provide you with a home like this."

"Why would you want to? We don't need two houses," she reasoned. "And I don't need money or things from you, Noah. I thought by now you understood that."

He fixed his gaze on the open doors and watched the leaves on a cottonwood tremble beneath the night breeze. The idea of loving Bella, of making a life with her, made him tremble the same way. Only his quaking was caused by fear, not by a cooling wind.

"A man wants to give to his woman, Bella. Not take."

"I don't consider myself wealthy, Noah. And I won't until I have a family of my own. That's wealth. Not houses or land or anything money can get you."

If she stuck with him, she'd remain a poor woman, Noah thought ruefully.

She reached over and placed a hand over his. "I've

not pressed you to talk about your past, Noah. But I think—well, I get the feeling you're still living there."

Everything inside him recoiled. "What makes you think that?"

"Because you're certainly not living for the future." The tips of her finger traced over his knuckles then down his wrist and onto his forearm. The cuts from the barbed wire were still stitched and covered with Band-Aids but she could have whacked the wounds with a rolling pin and the pain wouldn't come near to matching the empty feeling in his chest.

"I've already told you about my past."

"You've never told me about the years after you left your grandfather's place, before you came here. Was there a special woman in your life?"

"Why the hell would you want to know that?" he barked the question at her. Then before she could answer, he sat up on the side of the bed and pulled on his shorts.

"Because I care about you. Because I want to know the real reason you've hidden your heart behind a barrier of barbed wire."

"What if I don't want to tell you?" he asked bluntly.

She snorted. "If? It's already obvious you don't want to tell me anything. But I think I deserve a few answers, don't you?"

A feeling of inevitability came over him and he looked at her. "What do you want to hear? The good stuff? The part about where I finally found a family that I put my faith in and cared about? Or would you rather hear the bad? The part about people I trusted turning their backs on me?"

The bitterness in his voice should have been enough

to put her off, but it wasn't. Instead, she scooted closer and rested her hand on his bare knee.

"Why don't you tell me about all of it?" she suggested.

With a heavy sigh, he shook his head. "All right. Maybe you do need to hear this. Maybe then you'll see that I'm way too warped to give you the kind of love you deserve."

"Look, Noah, you can't get much worse than what Marcus did to me. Besides, nothing you can tell me is going to make me change my mind about you. You're a good man."

He swiped a hand over his face. "There's a few people down in Arizona who don't think so. And I figure the seven years I've been here hasn't changed their opinion."

"Why? Who are these people?"

"When I left the ranch near Benson I went to work on another ranch not far from Tombstone. A man named Ward Stevens owned Verde Canyon Ranch and almost from the first moment I met him I felt a kinship with the man. He didn't just own the ranch, but he also worked right along with the hands. He had more knowledge of horses and cattle in one finger than most of us will ever acquire in a lifetime."

"So you liked working for him?"

"It was like living a dream, Bella. The ranch covered an enormous area and though much of it was stark and wild, there were parts when the rains came that would turn beautiful and green. Ward liked my work and dedication and after a few years, he gave me the opportunity to buy into the ranch. My part was small, but it was a partnership nonetheless."

"That must have been very special for you."

"A moment ago when you talked about money not buying the important things, well, that's how I felt about Ward. He treated me like a son and I would've done anything for the man."

She squared around so that she was facing him. "So what happened? If everything was so good, why did you leave?"

"I had no choice," he said flatly. "Ward believed I was sleeping with his wife."

"And you couldn't reason with him?"

He made a cynical grunt. "Aren't you going to ask whether I was having an affair with the woman?"

"Why would I bother with a ridiculous question? I know you wouldn't do something like that. To a friend or an enemy."

Dropping his head in his hands, he wondered why she had to have so much faith in him. Where did all that trust come from? Especially after she'd had a cheating husband.

"Well, it wasn't true. Oh, Camilla had pursued me all right. She'd tried every trick in the book to seduce me, but I wasn't about to stab my friend in the back. Besides, at that time I had met a woman I was beginning to care about. I was even thinking of asking her to marry me. That's how much Ward's love and friendship had boosted my confidence. But that all went to hell."

"So what happened? How did it all end?"

He lifted his head and looked at her. "I made one last effort to reason with Camilla. I even threatened to go to Ward and tell him what she'd been up to. After that she became, I guess you'd call it, a scorned woman. To get back at me, she goes to Ward and tells him that I'd been after her. That for weeks I'd been trying to seduce her, but she'd resisted."

"And he believed her?"

"Every word. The more I tried to reason with the man, the angrier he got. He threatened to kill me if I didn't get off the ranch. By then I didn't have much choice in the matter. There wasn't any way to prove my innocence. So I sold my interest in the ranch back to Ward and left Verde Canyon."

"What about the woman you were planning to marry?"

The laugh that erupted from his throat tasted like bitter gall. "When she found out why Ward had run me off the ranch, she turned against me, too. She believed Camilla's story. Not mine."

Bella's head swung back and forth. "So you lost her, too," she said softly.

"I lost everything. Even my reputation. And that was the thing that bothered me the most. People around Tombstone had come to like and respect me. The ranch hands on the Verde had all treated me as their equal. I had finally lifted myself up and out of the broken life I'd had as a kid. But Camilla's lies wiped all of that away."

"I don't understand, Noah. Did Ward's wife seem like that sort of woman when you first went to work on the ranch?"

He shook his head. "Not at all. I never saw her so much as bat an eyelash at any man, other than her husband. She adored Ward, and he did her. He was quite a bit older than Camilla, but that didn't seem to be a problem. They both wanted children and she was having trouble conceiving. When she finally became pregnant they were so happy. Everybody was happy for them. And then when it was nearly time for the baby to be born something went wrong and she miscarried. For a long time afterward it was like a tomb around the house. The grief must have twisted something in her mind. I don't know. But she changed and for some reason looked at me as an escape from her problems."

"I suppose that's why everyone believed her. Because up until the tragedy with the baby, she'd always been a loving wife," Bella said thoughtfully. "So you left Verde Canyon and came here?"

"That's right. And I've never spoken to Ward or Camilla or anyone connected to Verde Canyon since." His expression grim, he looked at her. "See, Bella, I tried to love. I tried to be a part of a real family. It didn't work. I came away from the Verde more broken than I'd ever been before. I'm not about to let myself get into that vulnerable position again. It's not worth the pain."

She stared at him in stunned fascination. "Surely you can't equate all that happened in Arizona with me and you! There's no comparison!"

"Isn't there?" he asked caustically. "No, you're not Jett's wife, but you're his sister. One that he loves very dearly. What do you think he'd say or do if he discovered I'd been sleeping in your bed?"

Rising to her feet, she stood, her hands anchored on either side of her hips as she faced him. "Who I choose to sleep with is none of Jett's business. He'd tell you that himself. Furthermore, he respects you. I figure he'd probably shout, *Hallelujah, Bella finally has a man in her life*."

With a grunt of disbelief, he reached for his jeans. "You're looking at life through rose-colored glasses."

Her lips pressed to a thin, angry line. "Why? Because I let myself believe in someone? Love someone? You're the one who's looking through distorted lenses, Noah. You see everything in a dark and twisted way! I'm sure a few minutes ago after we made love, you were lying there wondering how long it would be before I stuck a knife in your back."

Standing, he stepped into his jeans and after zipping them up, snatched his shirt from the floor. "Can you blame me?"

She stared at him as though he'd slapped her. "Oh, Noah," she said softly, "don't you think it's time to put all that behind you?"

"That's easy for you to say, Bella. You didn't live through it."

Her jaw tight, she watched him snap his shirt and stuff the tails into his jeans. "You think I lived in a rose garden all my life? You think I didn't go through hell with Marcus? Oh, poor pitiful me. Oh, poor pitiful Noah. Life has been bad to both of us. So let's just give up and go cry in our beer. Is that what you want?"

He jerked on his boots, amazed that he'd been so hot to be with her, he'd not even taken the time to remove his spurs. That was a sure sign he was in deep trouble.

"I want you to leave me alone," he snapped. "Go find someone else to psychoanalyze."

"If I thought you meant that, I—"

"I do mean it!" he interrupted.

He stalked out of the bedroom, but she raced on his heels. "Where are you going? I thought you were planning on staying the night?"

"That isn't going to happen. Not tonight. Not again."

By now he was striding through the kitchen, intent on escaping through the back door.

As he snatched his hat from a wall peg and tugged it low on his forehead, she hurried up to his side.

"So you're going to run away," she accused. "Running and hiding from your feelings isn't going to fix anything. Besides that, I'm not going to let you take the coward's way out."

He couldn't believe that after all he'd said, after hearing the nasty story of Verde Canyon, she still refused to give up on him. A part of him wanted to call her a little fool. But the other part wanted to jerk her into his arms and never let her go.

"Don't waste your time on me, Bella. I don't want that. I want you to be happy."

Before she could try to stop him, he slipped out the door and hurried to the truck. But as he pulled away and headed toward the cabin, he wondered how much longer he could stay here on the J Bar S. How long would it be before Bella's pursuit forced him to quit the ranch and move on?

Two days later, on Saturday afternoon, Noah and Jett rode their horses through a large herd of steers located on the far west range of the ranch. Signs of the continuing drought were everywhere. Grass was scarce and in some instances even the sagebrush had succumbed to the lack of water.

Noah was studying a motley-colored steer standing near a patch of prickly pear when Jett reined his horse to a stop. Propping his forearm over the saddle horn, he looked toward the valley floor.

"I remember when that part of the ranch used to be green. Now it looks like someone has set a match to it," he said grimly. "Sassy doesn't want to sell anything with a hide or hooves and I've tried to keep that from happening. But I'm afraid there's not much left to do. Any chance of rain won't come until early winter and even then there's no guarantees."

"Yeah. It's a bad situation," Noah agreed. "But Sassy's

a sensible woman. If you decide to sell off half the steers, she'll understand you have no choice."

Jett sighed. "Yeah. But I hate to disappoint her. She thinks I'm some sort of miracle worker." With a wry smile slanting his lips, he looked over at Noah. "It's nice to have a woman put that much faith in you. But sometimes it awfully hard to live up to, you know?"

Noah lifted his hat from his head and swiped a hand through his damp hair. "I wouldn't know too much about that."

What are you lying for, Noah? Bella has put all kinds of misguided faith in you and you've done your best to let her down. When are you going to own up to the truth? When are you going to admit to yourself that you are a coward?

Noah could feel Jett's thoughtful gaze traveling over him and the scrutiny left him cold and sick. The same way he'd felt when he'd driven away from Bella's last Thursday night.

"Something is wrong with you," he said. "Spit it out."

Noah groaned. "Nothing is wrong. It's been damned hot today and I've been in the saddle for most of it."

"If there was ever a man that loves being atop a horse, no matter the weather, it's you. So try again. That one doesn't fly."

Noah drew in a bracing breath and blew it out. "I might as well talk to you about this now. I've been planning on it, anyway."

Jett's horse made a restless side step and he steered the animal back so that he was facing Noah. "You're having problems with the men," he said before Noah could begin. "I had a feeling Parker was going to cause trouble. He's got an attitude of sorts. But I thought you could deal with it."

Noah shook his head. "There's nothing wrong with Parker. He's a good worker. The men are fine. This is something else…a woman."

Jett's expression looked like a man who'd just been shot. "A woman! Are you kidding me?"

"I wish," he said glumly.

"Why? I think it's great! A woman is just what you've been needing."

The sick feeling boiling in the pit of Noah's stomach grew worse. "You won't think so, when I tell you who the woman is," he muttered.

"I doubt it. I can't imagine you getting hooked up with some floozy. You're too cautious for something like that. Tell me about her," Jett urged.

Deciding he couldn't put it off any longer, Noah glanced away from his friend and fixed his gaze back on the motley steer. The animal was now grazing on the prickly pear, chewing the green pads, spines and all. At the moment Noah felt as if he'd eaten a few cactus thorns himself.

"It's Bella."

Jett stared at him for long moments before a wide grin finally settled across his face. "You and Bella. I don't know why I hadn't thought of the two of you getting together, but I should have. You're perfect for each other. Damn, Noah, you've made me happy."

He'd expected Jett to be civil about the news, but not anything close to happy. "Hell, Jett, how long have you known me?"

"Close to seven years or something like that. Why?"

Frowning now, he stepped down from the saddle and stood next to his horse's head. The sorrel nudged him on the shoulder and Noah automatically pulled a peppermint candy from his pocket and gave it to the horse.

To Jett, he said, "You know what kind of man I am. I don't have much. And I don't want much. Give me a horse, a few cows to look after and a sky over my head and I'm satisfied. Is that the kind of man you think Bella needs in her life?"

"You're exactly the kind she needs."

"Damn, Jett, you need a vacation from your law office. You're not thinking straight. Bella doesn't need a man like me. I can't give her anything."

"If you're thinking my sister needs a man with money, then you're the one who's messed up. You can take away her loneliness. You can give her love and children and meaning to her life."

"And that's supposed to be easier than giving her financial security?" He shook his head. "No matter. I've already made it clear to Bella that I can't give her any of those things. I—don't plan on seeing her anymore."

The creak of Jett's saddle told Noah the man was dismounting long before he came to stand next to him.

"I hope you don't mean that," he said.

"I made it clear to Bella a few nights ago. But I don't think— Well, she believes she can change my mind. I won't."

Jett thoughtfully stroked his chin. "I'm getting the picture now. I thought she was upset over a case she's been working on. Instead, it's you that has her all down and out."

If possible, Noah felt even worse. "I'm sorry about that, Jett. I never wanted to hurt her. It's just that she—" He shook his head. "She's put me up on some damned pedestal where I don't belong."

"That's the special thing about having a woman love you, Noah. She'll look past your faults and see

the good. I thank God that each and every day Sassy
does it with me."

At one time, back on the Verde, Noah had believed
there was good in him. He'd worked hard to show everyone that he wasn't like his worthless father, or indif-
ferent, petty, narrow-minded grandfather. But Ward's
betrayal had cut Noah down. Now he told himself he
didn't give a damn what people thought of him. Not
even Bella.

"We better ride on to the windmill," Noah said,
abruptly changing the subject. "If it breaks down we'll
have some dying cattle on our hands."

Jett gave him an affectionate slap on the shoulder.
"Yeah. Let's mount up."

Chapter Nine

The next evening was Skyler's birthday party and though Bella wasn't in the mood for merrymaking, she couldn't miss her little niece's celebration.

Dressed in a red-and-white sundress, with her hair pulled into a messy bun, she drove to Jett and Sassy's to join the outdoor festivities.

She'd not been surprised to find a big crowd gathered at the back of the house, partaking of barbecued beef and all the trimmings, but she'd been a little put off by the handful of men who'd been trying to strike up a conversation with her from the moment she'd arrived.

"All right, dear brother," she said to Jett, once she had him cornered away from the crowd. "What do think you're trying to do? I'm not looking for a date or anything like it."

He glanced over his shoulder before giving her a sheepish look. "Bella, I'm not responsible for those guys. Sassy invited them over from the Horn. I didn't tell her that inviting Noah would be enough to make you happy."

Surprised, Bella stared at her brother. "How did you—"

"Noah brought it up. I think he had some sort of crazy idea that I wouldn't approve of the two of you together."

Rather than letting Jett see the sadness in her eyes, Bella looked down at the cup of punch she was holding. "I'm afraid Noah has some mixed-up notions about a lot of things."

"I thought he'd be here this evening. He adores Skyler."

"But he hates crowds." *And he doesn't want to be anywhere near me,* Bella could have told him. "I wouldn't look for him to show up."

"I think you might be wrong about that."

She looked up to see her brother's attention had turned toward a group of people standing beneath the covered portion of the patio. And then she caught sight of Noah among them. The sight of him dressed in a white Western shirt and dark jeans caused her heart to lurch with surprise and an immense sense of despair.

Before she could tear her gaze away from him, she spotted Skyler running up to him. He reacted to the child by scooping her up and balancing her in the crook of one arm. Bella's heart winced with bittersweet longing as she watched the little girl wrap her arms around Noah's neck.

He would be a wonderful father, Bella thought. Mainly because he knew all the things not to do.

"Looks like I was wrong about him coming to the party," she murmured.

Jett tossed her a knowing grin. "Obviously. I'd better go say hello. I don't imagine he'll stick around for very long."

"Uh, Jett, please don't bring up my name to him. Okay?"

"Why would I bother doing that? You're already on the guy's mind. Besides, you're here and he's here. It's an opportune time for you two to get together."

Noah didn't want to get together with her. That was the whole issue, she wanted to tell her brother. Instead, she simply nodded and said, "I see Reggie's wife and she has the baby with her. Maybe she'll let me hold him."

Before Jett could say more, Bella quickly headed across the yard to where Evita was sitting in a lawn chair holding her new son. She visited with the young woman and baby for several minutes before she eventually walked over to the refreshment table.

After ladling more punch into her plastic cup, she stepped back from the table and was scanning the crowd for a glimpse of Sassy when one of the Silver Horn ranch hands walked up to her.

In his late thirties and single, Denver was undeniably handsome with darkly tanned features and brown hair that was naturally streaked with gold. She'd often heard Jett speak of the man before and knew he was one of the huge ranch's top employees.

"Don't you need some cake to go along with your punch?" he asked with a lazy smile.

Not wanting to appear rude, she smiled back at him. "No thanks. I've already had a giant piece. I'd better stop with it."

He picked up a foam saucer and piled several pieces

of pecans and candied mints on it, then stood beside Bella and began to eat the snack.

"It's a nice evening for a party," he remarked. "Not a cloud in the sky. But I imagine Jett wouldn't have minded to see a few rain clouds gathering."

"Rain would be a blessed relief for everyone." She glanced at him and wondered why she couldn't feel a spark of interest. Why did her heart have to be hung up on a dark, brooding cowboy who wanted to keep pushing her away? "What do you do on the Horn?" she asked politely.

"I oversee the cow/calf operation. I work closely with Rafe, the foreman. I expect you know him."

She smiled faintly. "Jett has been the Horn's lawyer for years and he's married to a Calhoun, so I'm fairly familiar with the entire family."

He said, "I hear you're a lawyer, too."

Bella wondered if Sassy had been discussing her with this man. The notion should've irked her, but it didn't. Sassy was a romantic and she wanted Bella's life to be rich with love and children. Bella supposed she was going to have to confide in Sassy soon. Her sister-in-law needed to know that Bella was locked in a one-sided love affair and that dangling a bunch of bachelors in front of her was pointless.

"That's right. But it will be a long time before I gain the experience Jett has."

"I'm—" Denver's next words suddenly faltered as something behind her caught his attention.

In the next instant, a familiar hand wrapped around her upper arm and Bella realized Noah was the cause of the interruption.

"Sorry, Denver," he said bluntly. "I need to speak with Bella privately."

Her mouth fell open as he quickly led her away from Denver and didn't stop until they were in the front yard, hidden from view by a thick stand of aspen trees.

"What are you—"

Before she could finish the question, her back was pressed against a tree trunk and his lips were devouring hers in a kiss that was spinning her head in a drunken whirl.

"What do you think you're doing?" he asked when he finally lifted his head away from hers.

She sucked in a ragged breath and blew it out. "I was about to ask you the very same thing!"

His nostrils were pinched, the corners of his mouth tight as his blue gaze sliced over her face. And then, just as suddenly his grip on her shoulders eased and he was shaking his head with self-contempt. "Dear God, I've gone crazy! Seeing you with Denver—something snapped in me."

Amazed, she stared at him. "You haven't so much as spoken to me this evening," she said in a voice that was both angry and hurt. "This display of jealousy seems out of place, don't you think? Especially when you told me the other night to go find some other man. Or have you forgotten?"

He took a step back and in spite of being annoyed with him, Bella wanted to grab the front of his shirt and tug him back to her. Which made her thinking just as crazy as his.

"I've not forgotten anything, Bella." He turned aside and stared across the ranch yard, to the barns and corrals where he started and ended his workdays. "And I'm sorry. Again. Hell, that's all I seem to be able to do, isn't it? Apologize for being a jerk."

He looked so tall and strong, so achingly handsome

standing there in his white shirt and black hat pulled low on his forehead. Moments earlier, when she'd been crushed in the circle of his arms, she'd caught a faint whiff of masculine cologne. Before this evening, her Noah had never smelled of anything more than horses and hay and leather. The added scent of sandalwood and sweet grasses made her realize she'd never seen him dressed to go out. The two of them had never been off the ranch together.

The fact might have annoyed another woman, but not Bella. It filled her with excitement to think there was still so much she had yet to learn about this man, so much the two of them could do together. If he'd only give them a chance.

Finally, she said, "I don't want your apology, Noah. I just want you."

He swallowed, then slowly turned back to her. "I'm beginning to see that my days here are numbered."

"What does that mean?"

"It means the only way I can end this obsession I have for you is to leave here."

His answer whammed her like a slap in the face. He thought of her as an obsession while she considered him her love, her life. He was intent on building a canyon between them. Just like the one he'd warned her about riding down.

With tears stinging the back of her eyes, she wrapped her hand around his forearm. "I'm not going to let that happen."

His features were as rigid as a rock mask. "How are you going to stop me? Threaten me, like Camilla did?"

God help her to keep from slapping his face, she prayed. "That chip on your shoulder is growing bigger and uglier. And frankly, I'm getting sick of looking at it. Somebody needs to knock the damned thing off. And I figure Denver could get the job done."

His gray eyes turned to twin blazes. "Like hell!"

Goading him in this way might be wrong of her, Bella thought, but if he wanted to play dirty, then she could, too. "Oh, I don't know, he looks pretty strong to me."

"Strong," he repeated, his soft voice full of danger. "Is that what you want from me?"

Just as she started to answer, he hooked an arm around her waist and jerked her forward. She toppled against him and he used the close proximity to cover her mouth with his.

The contact created an instant combustion and with a groan of sweet surrender, Bella's arms circled tightly around him, and her tongue invited his to join hers in a slow, sensual dance. The words they'd flung at each other no longer mattered. Noah was kissing her, holding her, and for the moment that was enough.

If not for the sound of a nearby vehicle firing to life, the hot embrace might have gone on and on. Instead, they broke apart and Noah quickly stepped back.

Bella gulped for air and tried to stem the shaking in her legs. "Some of the guests must be leaving the party," she voiced the obvious.

"Yeah. And as soon as I say goodbye to Jett and Sassy, I'll be leaving, too. You go on back to Denver. He's the kind of man you need. Not me."

When he walked away, Bella didn't try to stop him. In his present state of mind, it would be useless to try to reason with him. One second he was jealously jerking her away from Denver and the next he was telling her to go back to him. Even if she was a psychiatrist, she couldn't figure his hot and cold behavior. But one thing she did know. She had to use everything in her power to keep him on the J Bar S. Otherwise, her chance for a life with him would be over.

Late Monday afternoon, at an outdoor restaurant not far from Bella and Jett's office building, she sat at a small wrought-iron table, sipping on a cup of Columbian coffee and nibbling at a chocolate biscotti. Aaron Potter, the man sitting across from her, had graying dark hair and a wide affable face. His blue summer-weight suit was rumpled and the knot of his tie slightly askew, but as he talked she got the feeling he was good at his job and that gave her a measure of confidence as she headed closer to Brent Stanhope's trial.

"I'm very grateful to you for meeting me like this," she told him. "Frankly, I had reached a point where I didn't know what direction to take next. My gut feeling is that the husband has hidden the missing jewelry somewhere and plans to collect the insurance on it. The other jewelry is what he used to plant in Brent's car."

"And what was the husband's motive for framing his gardener? From what he tells me, he likes Brent. They've even gone to sporting events together."

This little café was normally one of Bella's favorites. And at this time of the evening, she was usually craving a dose of caffeine and sugar, but since her exchange with Noah at the party yesterday, she'd not wanted to eat or drink anything. And focusing on her work had become a major effort. She had to think of some way to make him see reason, but so far her jumbled thoughts had reached a blank.

"When I spoke with the wife, I got the feeling her husband had warned her not to talk. I also got the impression he controls her with physical threats—if you know what I mean. Brent's a nice-looking young guy. I got the feeling jealousy was the motive in this case."

"Hmm. Sounds reasonable. But a jury would argue that the husband could have simply fired the guy to get rid of him. He didn't need to go to the trouble of framing him with theft."

Bella nodded. "That's true. But the husband saw an opportunity to kill two birds with one stone. Get rid of Brent completely and make some money to boot."

A look of disgust came over the investigator's face. "About three years ago, this guy collected on an expensive vehicle. The insurance company couldn't prove he'd set the fire that turned the car into a piece of tinfoil, but I'd bet my savings account he was guilty then and he's guilty now."

"But how do you get evidence against him?"

"I have my ways, Ms. Sundell. One being to put a tail on the wife and husband and see what turns up. In the meantime, if your client can think of anything that might shed some light on where the jewelry might be stashed, then let me know." He pulled a card from his wallet and pushed it across the table to her. "In case you need to contact me after hours here's my home phone and address."

"Thank you, Mr. Potter."

After she tucked the card away in her handbag, the two of them continued to discuss the case for a few more minutes before they departed the café.

Bella walked slowly back to the Sundell law office, her thoughts vacillating from the Stanhope case to Noah. When she entered the waiting area, Peta looked up from her work.

"Glad you're back," she said. "Jett wants to see you. I don't know what it's about, but he looked concerned."

"Thanks, Peta. I'll go right in."

After putting her handbag and briefcase in her office, she quickly headed over to Jett's office. She found her brother standing over his desk, gathering papers to take home with him.

"I just now got back from my meeting with the insurance investigator," she told him. "Peta said you wanted to see me."

Nodding, he pointed to a short couch positioned along the back wall of the room. "Let's sit down. I have something to show you."

Suddenly her heart was hammering with heavy dread. Had Noah made good on his threat and told Jett he was quitting his job as foreman of the J Bar S? She couldn't let him leave! Not without her!

Feeling dizzy with fear, Bella headed to the couch. A moment later, Jett joined her. A long business-sized envelope was in his hand.

"This came in my mail today."

Without any more explanation, he handed the envelope to her and as Bella read the address, she could feel the blood draining from her face.

"Jett, this is addressed to Noah in care of you. Why are you showing it to me?"

A clever smile slanted his lips. "Noah talked to me about the two of you. So I figured you should be the one to give him the letter. It will give you a good excuse to see him."

Ignoring the envelope in her hand, she squeezed her eyes shut. "I guess he told you that he—doesn't want us to be together anymore."

Jett sighed. "Noah is a little misguided. But he'll come around."

"I'm not so certain," she said in a strained voice,

then opening her eyes, she looked hopelessly at her brother. "Jett, he's talking about leaving. And all because of me. If that happened you'd be losing the best ranch hand you've ever had. And I—well, I can't even bear to think about him being gone."

Seeing her anguish, Jett put a reassuring hand on her shoulder. "Look, Bella, don't worry about me losing my foreman. From the day I hired Noah, I could see he was way overqualified for the job. He should be running a ranch of his own. He knows it and I know it. Something, I don't know what, is keeping him in limbo. But I don't push the matter with him, frankly because he's not the kind of man you can push. And in the end, I guess I'm selfish. I like having him here."

He pointed to the letter in her hand. "Do you have any idea of what this might be about?"

Bella's gaze dropped from her brother to the return address on the envelope. Camilla Ward, Tombstone, Arizona. "Oh! Oh, no!"

"Bella, what's wrong? Do you know the person who sent this letter?"

Completely stunned, she stared blindly at floor. "No. Not exactly. I mean, he's talked to me about this person before. But I have no idea why he'd be getting a letter from her."

Jett sighed. "Well, Noah has worked for me for seven years and he's never received mail through my office. Apparently this person wanted to make sure he received it."

"I'm wondering how she found him?" Bella voiced the question out loud. "He broke ties with her years ago."

Frowning, Jett asked, "Is she an ex-wife or something?"

The clenched knot in Bella's stomach worked its way

up to lodge in her throat. "No. She's— I guess you could call her one of Noah's worst nightmares."

Long seconds ticked away as Jett thoughtfully studied the envelope in Bella's hand. Finally, he said, "If you want to tear that thing up, I'll pretend I didn't see it."

"Is that advice coming from a brother or a lawyer?" she asked dubiously.

"That wasn't advice. Just a brotherly suggestion."

Tearing up the letter and pretending she'd never seen it was tempting. After all of the loss and pain Camilla Ward had caused Noah, it would be an act of mercy to keep her from inflicting more. But Bella wasn't a deceitful or manipulating person. If she ever hoped to have a future with Noah, it had to be built on honesty.

"Thanks, Jett, but I couldn't live with that. And the more I think about this, the more I believe he needs to see it."

"So he can stick a match to it and put it all behind him once and for all? That kind of thing?"

She swallowed as apprehension coiled her nerves even tighter. "Exactly."

Jett glanced at his watch. "If you hurry, you might catch Noah before he leaves the ranch yard."

Noah didn't want to see her for any reason. How was he going to react when she showed him this letter? She couldn't worry about that now, she thought, as she hurried out of Jett's office. She could only hope that whatever Camilla Ward had to say would finally put an end to Noah's bitter memories.

Back at the J Bar S ranch yard, Noah was squatted at the front of a chestnut horse, running both hands gently over the animal's left cannon bone. There was a small amount of swelling in the tendon, but no obvious bump.

"I don't like the heat I'm feeling. Lead him down the alleyway, Lew," he told the young ranch hand, "so I can see how he's tracking."

He was intent on watching the horse's movements for any sign of lameness when he heard a light step behind him. Expecting it to be Sassy returning from her check on the mustangs, he didn't bother to look over his shoulder. Instead, he kept his focus on the horse's gait until Lew led the horse in a wide arc, then brought him back to where Noah was standing at the entrance of the horse barn.

"He's out of the remuda for now," Noah told cowboy. "Tie him to the hitching post out front and I'll bring the trailer around. Maybe Doc can make a quick diagnosis. In the meantime, put Coco in the catch pen with the rest of the herd. You can ride him tomorrow."

"Will do," Lew said, then added, "If you have something else you need to do I can take Sweet Potato over to the Horn."

"Thanks, Lew, but I can manage. You have a long drive home."

Lew darted a glance at something behind Noah, then with a shrug led the horse past him. "Whatever you say."

Noah turned with intentions of going to fetch the truck and trailer to van Sweet Potato over to the Horn. But two steps in that direction were as far as he got.

Bella was standing just inside the wide-open doorway of the barn. A close-fitting blue dress hugged her luscious curves and stopped just at the top of her knees. Her dark hair was pulled into a neat coil at the back of her head, while a pair of red high heels covered her feet.

She looked beautiful and sexy, but very unlike herself. Not because she was dressed as a career woman, but because a smile was missing from her face. And suddenly he was wondering if she'd stopped by the ranch to finally end things with him. Maybe his unreasonable behavior at the party yesterday had finally opened her eyes and she'd decided he was someone she didn't want in her life. The idea made him sick to his stomach. Yet it was inevitable and for the best.

"Hello, Noah," she greeted him. "Do you have a minute or two?"

"I was just headed over to the Horn," he told her, glad that he had a legitimate excuse to keep their conversation brief.

"This is very important. I have something to give you."

Her unexpected words had him moving closer. "Give me," he repeated inanely. "What—"

She inclined her head toward the open door of the feed room. "Let's go in there. This is rather private."

Being cooped up with her in a small space was the last thing Noah needed, but she didn't give him time to argue the point. She'd already turned away from him and headed into the feed room. That's when Noah noticed she was holding a white envelope behind her back.

Totally confused, Noah strode after her and followed her into the dimly lit room filled with sacks of grain, alfalfa hay and tubs of supplements.

When she came to a stop in the middle of the room, Noah stood a few steps away, his back resting against a stack of sacked bran.

"What is this all about?" Noah asked.

"You'll have to answer that," she said. "This letter came for you today at the office. It was sent in care of Jett."

Noah didn't get letters. Not the personal kind. His

rural mailbox, erected at the main entrance to the ranch, was usually full of junk mail, or a random bill.

"Must be a mistake. I don't correspond with anyone."

She came to stand directly in front of him and Noah couldn't help but notice the piece of paper was trembling as she handed it over.

"Maybe not. But someone is trying to correspond with you."

He flipped the envelope around and immediately felt like someone had kicked him in the teeth. Camilla!

His first instinct was to throw the piece of mail to the floor and grind his heel into it. But shock kept him from making any sort of move.

Finally, he managed to ask, "Why didn't Jett give this to me? He's usually home before I leave the ranch yard."

"My brother thought I should be the one to give it to you. He doesn't understand that you view me as a contagious disease," she added cynically.

Biting back a curse, he thrust the envelope back at her. "You wasted your time delivering this piece of garbage. Take it. Throw it away."

Her eyes widened with disbelief. "You don't intend to open it?"

"Why the hell should I? That woman ruined my life. Seven years have passed since I left Tombstone. What could she possibly be saying now that could mean a damned thing to me?"

Bella shook her head. "It must've been important to her. She obviously went to a lot of trouble to track you down."

"Like I should care," he sneered.

She studied him with dark expectant eyes and he realized she was expecting him to face this thing like a man. Not a coward.

Running and hiding from your feelings isn't going to fix anything.

Bella's words continued to roll through his mind, taunting and daring him to face the painful memories that had haunted him for all these years.

With a groan of surrender, he ripped the mail open, then handed the contents to her. "Please read it to me, would you?"

Uncertainty crossed her face as she glanced from the letter to him. "Are you sure? Maybe you should read this privately," she suggested.

"No. Whatever the woman has to say I want you to hear, too."

Nodding solemnly, she unfolded the stationery and began to read.

Dear Noah,
This letter is to sadly inform you of Ward's recent death. For the past two years his health had steadily declined, and heartbreaking as it was for me, he welcomed the end.

I understand I have no right to ask you for anything, but I need for you to come to Verde Canyon as soon as possible. There's much we need to discuss.
Camilla.

Ward, dead!
Completely stunned, Noah moved a few steps over and sat down on a low stack of hay. "I can't believe it, Bella. Ward would've only been in his late fifties!"

She stepped over and placed a comforting hand on his shoulder. "I'm so sorry, Noah. I think—well, in spite of everything that happened with the two of you, I know how this must hurt."

Amazed that she could understand something that was only beginning to register with him, he looked up at her. "Why does it hurt, Bella?" he asked hoarsely. "I thought I hated the man."

"He wounded you deeply and that was your way of coping. Believing you hated him took some of the pain away."

An utter sense of loss welled up in him and before she could see the sting of tears in his eyes, he dropped his head and swallowed hard. "I just wish he hadn't gone to his grave believing I'd wronged him."

"Maybe he didn't."

Frowning now, he lifted his head. "Isn't it obvious? Camilla didn't write until after he was gone."

"There could be all sorts of reasons why you're hearing from her now instead of before the man died. That's why you have to go to Verde Canyon and see her. To find out exactly why she wants to see you."

He shot to his feet and began to pace around the dusty room. "Are you crazy? That woman caused me nothing but misery. She not only ripped apart a friendship, she tore down everything good I had built to that point in my life. Face her again? Hell no!"

He didn't realize Bella had caught up to him until she wrapped a hand around his forearm. "What are you afraid of? She can't hurt you now. Or are you worried you might run into your old girlfriend? The one you were thinking of marrying? Maybe her desertion bothered you much more than the debacle with Camilla and Ward."

He frowned with disbelief. "Do you honestly think that?"

She shrugged one shoulder. "I don't know what to think. The way I see it, neither one of these women should be striking a chord of fear in you, but it looks like they are. You're afraid to travel down to Arizona."

Groaning with frustration, he shook his head. "Kelsey was just a girlfriend. It's true I was considering asking her to marry me. But now that I've had years to think about it, I can see that notion wasn't prompted by love. It was because she was the first woman with any class to show me some respect and I was grateful more than anything. The fact that she lost faith in me probably turned out to be a good thing. Even if I had gotten around to proposing to her, I doubt a marriage between us would've lasted a year."

"Then if it's not her that's keeping you from going, it has to be Camilla."

"Damn it, Bella, it's not her! Not exactly. She was never anything more to me than a friend. And after she went crazy, I didn't even consider her to be that much. It's just that the whole place—the Verde—I loved it with all my heart. I don't know that I can bear seeing the ranch again."

She squeezed his arm. "I'll go with you, Noah. We'll go together."

"Why would you want to do that? This is my baggage. My problem."

A tender expression came over her features as she slid her arms around his waist and snuggled the front of her body to his. "Oh, Noah," she said softly, "you should know by now that I love you. I don't want to share only good times with you. I want to share the troubled times, too."

Noah's heart was aching to put his arms around her, to hold on tight and never let go. But he couldn't let pain sway him. "No. You have some misguided notion that I'm a good man. Good enough for you, that is. And you're wrong."

"And you have the foolish notion that you can control what my heart feels for you. But you can't, Noah. No more than you can control what your heart is trying to say to you."

His jaw clamped tight, he moved away from her tempting body and turned his back to her. "I'm not going to Tombstone, Bella. We're not going. Ward is dead. Everything is dead. Over. Why can't you get that through your head?"

"Nothing is over, Noah. It's just now beginning. Pretty soon you're going to wake up and see that for yourself. When you do, you know where to find me."

He was trying to think of some way to shoot down her comments when he heard her high heels clicking past him and out the door of the feed room.

Glancing around, he spotted the letter still lying where Bella had laid it on the hay bale. He walked over and stuffed it and the envelope in his shirt pocket, then strode quickly out of the feed room.

Sweet Potato was waiting at the hitching rail. He couldn't stop to think about Ward's death or Camilla's request for him to return to the Verde. And he especially couldn't let himself dwell on thoughts of Bella.

But as he jumped the lame horse into the trailer and headed toward the Silver Horn, three little words continued to revolve around and around in his head until they settled smack in the middle of his heart.

I love you.

What was he going to do now? Leave for Tombstone with Bella in tow? Or leave the J Bar S and Bella behind?

Chapter Ten

By the time Friday rolled around Bella still hadn't heard a word from Noah, although she'd learned through Jett that Noah had shared the contents of the letter with him and explained what had transpired seven years ago on Verde Canyon Ranch.

For the past few days since they'd talked in the feed room, she'd been hoping and praying that he would come to the conclusion that traveling to Arizona and facing Camilla was the best way to start his life over and begin a new one with Bella.

She'd told him that she loved him and maybe that had been a mistake. He'd just learned that his old friend was dead and that Camilla wanted to see him. No doubt he'd been too shocked for his mind to register much. But he'd had days to think about it now, she reasoned as she shut down the computer on her desk.

You might as well face it, Bella. Noah doesn't want

to start his life over with you. He doesn't care whether you love him or not. The only thing he ever wanted from you was sex and now even that is over. So move on and forget the man.

Bella was trying to shut down the voice in her head, when Jett suddenly walked into her office carrying a bouquet of red tulips.

Trying her best to give him a cheerful smile, she asked, "You're giving Sassy flowers tonight? What's the occasion?"

"These aren't for Sassy, though God knows she deserves to get flowers every day," he said. "These are for you, dear sis. I know you like red so I picked these."

"Picked them yourself, huh? Right from the flower shop?" she teased, then shook her head. "Why am I getting flowers? Do I look like I need something to perk me up?"

He placed the flowers on the corner of her desk, then leaned down to brush a kiss on her pale cheek. "Frankly, you've been looking awful."

Sighing, she switched off the lamp on her desk. "Thanks. Every girl wants to hear that."

He regarded her with a keen eye and Bella knew he was thinking about bringing up the subject of Noah. But thankfully, he didn't. Instead, he said, "The flowers are to say congratulations for getting Brent Stanhope exonerated of all charges."

Smiling wanly she rose to her feet and gathered a stack of case folders for Peta to file away. "I can't take the credit for that, Jett. Mr. Potter figured it out."

"Not without your help," he said knowingly. "You're the one who pulled the truth out of the wife."

Yesterday Bella had decided to talk with the woman again and her persistence had paid off. Rather than making threats, she'd appealed to the woman's fears and pointed out that her penalty for aiding her husband in a crime would be much less if she would confess. Thankfully, the woman had finally relented and admitted her husband had planned the whole scheme. As a result, the insurance investigator had caught him trying to sell the missing jewelry at a pawn shop in Las Vegas.

"Well, I'm just glad Brent is free and his record is cleared." She pointed to a gold-colored box on the corner of her desk. "Valerie sent me a card and chocolates. Along with a promise to take me out to dinner. Needless to say, she's happy."

Jett curled his arm around her shoulders and hugged her to his side. "I'm proud of you, sis. I only wish I could see a happy smile on your face. A real one."

"Don't worry about me, Jett. I'm not going to fall apart." Not yet, at least. But her heart was definitely close to cracking right down the middle.

"Noah is going to come around, sis. I don't have to tell you he's a man who holds things inside. He's needs time to digest everything that's happened."

Sighing, she said, "I'm beginning to think it's just not meant for me to have a husband and family. What am I doing wrong, Jett? After Marcus I waited so long to even let myself think of getting into another relationship. Now I've fallen in love with a man who's determined to be a bachelor for the rest of his life."

Before Jett could make a reply, she crossed the room and plucked the sweater she'd worn to work this morning from its hanger and tossed it over her arm.

When she returned to the desk and picked up the bouquet of tulips, Jett said, "Right now Noah doesn't believe he's good enough to be your husband."

Frustration boiled over, making her glare at her

brother. "What is it with you men and your egos?" She waved her hand in dismissive fashion. "Don't bother trying to answer that. It doesn't matter. I'm damned tired of trying to stroke Noah's, to try to pump him up and make him believe in himself! If he can't believe in himself, then why the hell am I wasting my time with him?"

She started toward the door, then realizing she'd forgotten her handbag, returned to her desk and collected it from the kneehole.

"Where are you going?" Jett asked.

She slung the strap of her handbag over her shoulder. "Home. Do you mind?" she asked sharply.

"I'm not your boss, Bella. You can do whatever you please. But don't you think Noah is the one you should be yelling this stuff at? Instead of me?"

Jett's questions brought her up short and with a rueful groan she shook her head. "I'm sorry, Jett. I shouldn't have gone off on you like that. I'm behaving like a shrew. And none of this is your fault. It's all mine."

"Forget it, sis. I already have."

With a grateful little smile, she kissed his cheek. "I'm going home and saddling up Casper. I've not given him any exercise in a while. Maybe the fresh air will help clear my head."

"Good idea. Just be sure and take a raincoat with you. The weatherman predicted a shower today."

Laughing now, Bella headed to the door. "Now, that is funny. Rain in June? After months of drought? You were listening to a fantasy, dear brother. Not a weather report."

"Just humor me and tie a slicker on your saddle. Okay?"

"Okay. Whatever you say."

* * *

Later that evening, Noah and two other ranch hands were standing just inside the door of the barn, waiting for the downpour of rain to slack enough to finish the barn chores.

"I don't think it's going to slow down," Reggie spoke above the roar of the rain pelting against the tin roof.

"I'm with you on that," Lew agreed. "And I don't want to stand here for hours. Let's drag out the slickers and finish the feeding."

"Don't complain, guys," Noah said, "this means more grass and less time spreading hay."

With good-natured grumbling, the two men left to fetch the slickers from the tack room. Noah remained standing at the door's edge, watching the rivulets of water creating tiny creeks across the packed ground in front of the barn. Lightning continued to crackle close by and Noah thought about the horses they'd turned out to pasture earlier that morning. Instinct would have them running straight for the shelter of the trees. Hopefully, the lightning would spare them.

Just as Reggie and Lew were returning with the slickers, Jett caught the faint sound of his cell phone ringing. As he pulled it from his pocket to answer, he stepped backward, hoping to lessen the din of the rain.

"Yes, Jett, it's raining here," he said before the other man had a chance to say anything. "We're going to have grass now, buddy!"

"The rain is a welcome sight," Jett agreed, "except that it has me worried."

"Can't do anything about the lightning, Jett. Just pray the cattle and horses don't get hit."

"It's not the livestock I'm worried about. It's Bella. She left work early with intentions of riding Casper.

I warned her to take a slicker, but I never expected a storm like this. Otherwise I would've told her not to go!"

Noah felt like an icy north wind just whammed him in the face. "She probably has her cell phone with her. Have you tried calling?"

Jett blew out an impatient breath. "For the past thirty minutes. My calls are going straight to her voice mail. I've been ringing her landline, too, but no answer there, either. Are you still at the ranch yard?"

"Yeah. We still have a few chores here."

"Oh, I thought maybe with the rain you'd already headed home and spotted her along the way."

"Don't worry, Jett. I'm going to go look for her."

"Noah, that would be like searching for a rabbit in a field of rose hedge! When Bella goes riding it's not just a little five-minute jaunt from the house and five back. She might go for miles. Especially considering the mood she was in!"

Jett's last remark caught Noah's attention, but he didn't press the other man to explain. There wasn't time for that. Besides, Noah had been in a hell of a mood himself for the past few days.

"I said don't worry," Noah clipped. "I have an idea where she might've gone. I'll call you as soon as I find her."

He abruptly ended the call and turned to see Lew and Reggie walking up the alleyway of the barn. He hurried to meet them and snatched one of the oiled dusters thrown over Lew's shoulder.

As he jammed his arms into the sleeves, he said, "Sorry, guys. An emergency has come up and I have to leave. You two handle things here."

Reggie asked, "Don't you need our help?"

Already in a run out of the barn, Noah yelled, "I'll call you if I do."

Once the dirt road passed the main ranch house, it was rough and rocky, but today with water already washing out ruts and dislodging boulders, the track was downright treacherous. Noah tried to go as fast as possible, but every few feet he was forced to downshift and jerk the steering wheel one way and then the other.

All the while he negotiated the truck over the rough terrain, icy fear continued to grow inside him. If Bella had ridden down the canyon, a flash flood could have swept her and Casper away. But even if she wasn't in the canyon, lightning was cracking all across the mesa. Even if it didn't strike her and the horse directly, it could definitely cause a tree to crash down on them.

What are you getting all panicky about, Noah? Other than being your boss's sister, she's nothing special to you. If she'd been that special, you would've already told her so. You would've confessed to her that she was the very beat of your heart. And you certainly wouldn't keep pushing her away.

Cursing at the mocking voice in his head, Noah twisted the windshield wipers to the fastest speed and hunched forward in an effort to see through the downpour. If Bella was out there, he'd have hell seeing her like this, he thought grimly.

Nothing is over, Noah. It's just now beginning. Pretty soon you're going to wake up and see that for yourself. When you do, you know where to find me.

These past few days Bella's words had been haunting him, making him wonder if he was a selfish bastard, a complete fool, or both. Now he was getting the uneasy feeling that she was right. His eyes were opening, but at the moment he didn't know where to find her.

By the time he reached Bella's house, Noah had failed to spot her or any sign of Casper's hoofprints in the muddy road. After a quick glance around, he headed to a garage built on the far end of the house. Her car was parked inside, so she'd clearly made it all the way home.

At the back door, he pounded loudly. "Bella? Are you in there?"

After a few moments passed with no response, he hurried to the barn. Mary Mae was dry and safe in one of the stalls, while Casper was nowhere to be seen. Noah was certain Bella would never stall one horse and leave the other in the pasture, so that meant she was still out in the storm somewhere. And the only way to find her was to saddle up and start searching.

A few minutes later, he reined the bay mare away from the barn and down a dim trail leading south. With heavy rain falling for more than an hour, there was no chance of spotting the tracks Casper had made when Bella rode away from the barn. Noah could merely guess and hope he was on the right path. But something deep in his gut told him she'd ridden to the canyon.

He'd warned her not to ride there alone. Besides the terrain being extremely rough, flash flooding could occur in a matter of minutes. But Bella didn't exactly follow his advice, he thought ruefully. In her opinion, he was overly cautious and too worried about something going wrong to let himself enjoy the pleasures of life. And perhaps he did approach everything with caution. Even loving her.

We've gone through this before, Noah, you don't love Bella. You love taking her to bed, that's all.

Then why the hell was he out here, in the middle of a violent thunderstorm, searching for her? Streaks of lightning were exploding over his head. Rain was pelting his face and turning the brim of his hat into a waterfall. He wasn't out here just because he enjoyed her warm, giving body, he thought desperately. No, Bella had become precious to him. So precious that if anything happened to her, his world would be nothing more than a black abyss.

After what seemed like an eternity, he reached the rim of the canyon and continued to travel along the edge until he found a spot he considered safe enough to descend the steep wall. But Mary Mae had other ideas and refused to take the path he'd chosen. Deciding she probably had more sense than he did about such things, he gave the mare her head and before long she found a crevice in the canyon rim wide enough for the two of them to pass through.

Patting her neck, he encouraged the courageous mare forward. "Good girl! Now see if you can get us to the bottom safely."

A half mile on down the canyon, Bella and Casper were perched on a narrow shelf of earth. Less than three feet beneath them, churning, muddy water raced over the canyon floor, carrying tumbleweeds, broken limbs and old logs. Small willow trees and bushes of sage bent beneath the force of the current and Bella realized if the rain continued to fall at this rate, the water would rise quickly and become even more dangerous.

Earlier this afternoon, when the rain had first started, she'd donned her slicker and turned around to head for home. But the storm had intensified very quickly. She'd tried to shelter beneath a small copse of evergreens and call Jett to give him her location and assure him she was on her way home. But the weather had knocked out the signal, making her phone useless.

Now the narrow shelf where she stood hunched next to Casper was only a temporary refuge. She needed to get herself and the horse out of the canyon. But even if she led the horse, rather than ride him, the bank behind them was far too steep and muddy for either of them to make the climb. That meant her only choice was to try to ford the water until she could find a place to climb to safety.

Oh God, she should've listened to Jett's prediction of rain. And she definitely should've heeded Noah's warning not to ride alone in the canyon. But for the past few days the constant ache in her chest had worn her down and the wild beauty of the canyon had started to call her. It was the one place where she could stop her mind from spinning long enough to really contemplate what was important in her life and what baggage she needed to throw away.

Before the storm had hit, she'd been thinking how much she loved Noah and how much he'd brought to her life. Earlier today, when she'd been talking to Jett, she'd lost her patience and her temper. But now, with rain streaming into her eyes and bolts of electricity dancing around her, she realized that no matter what Noah said, or if he went so far as to leave the J Bar S, she wasn't going to give up on him or the hope of them being together.

God willing she made it out of this flash flood, she was going straight to his cabin and she wasn't going to leave until he agreed to go with her to Arizona. He'd left his wounded heart there. And until he got it back, there was no hope he'd ever give her a piece of it.

Suddenly there was a flash directly across the span of rushing water and she looked up just in time to see a huge pine splitting down the middle. Fire blazed along the trunk, while ear-deafening thunder echoed through the canyon.

Terrified, Casper jumped backward. Bella screamed and stared in horror as the horse's back feet teetered on the edge of the solid ground.

"Whoa, boy! Whoa!" Knowing she had to appear strong and reassuring to the horse, she firmly pulled him forward until he was safely back to the center of the ledge. Then gently stroking his neck, she pressed her cheek against his. "It's okay, big guy. We're going to get out of this."

Casper nickered as though he understood what she was saying and then she realized his ears had gone on point, telling her he'd spotted something out there in the storm.

Turning, she stared through the white wall of rain, blinking at the rivulets running into her eyes. She could see nothing. But then she heard the faint sound of another horse answering Casper's call.

Could it be coming from a wild herd of mustangs seeking shelter from the storm, or had someone actually come looking for her?

By the time the horses exchanged another whinny, Bella spotted a horse and rider slowly making their way along the side of the north canyon wall. The muddy water churned all the way to the horse's knees and not far from the rider's stirrups.

Oh, God! It was Noah on Mary Mae!

More terrified than she'd ever been in her life, she watched the two of them slowly making their way toward her and Casper. There was no way of predicting if the mare's next step might take them into a deep hole or if she might walk straight into a boulder. Either way, Noah would probably be jolted from the saddle and into the churning water. The mare would bolt and end up in even more danger.

Why was he risking himself like this? Why hadn't he called the county rescue unit and let them take care of her? Could she dare hope it was because he might actually love her?

"Casper, the storm has made me delirious," she said to the horse. "I'm not thinking straight!"

Long, tense minutes passed before Noah finally got close enough to call out to her. By then it was all Bella could do to keep her tears at bay.

"Bella, are you okay?"

"I'm fine," she called back to him. "Just wet. I don't know how Casper and I are going to get out of here."

"You're going to have to ride out. The way Mary Mae and I came in."

Bella had always thought of herself as brave, but when she looked at the swirling water below her, she could feel her knees begin to quake.

"I'm not sure I can. The ground was barely covered with water when I jumped Casper onto the ledge. I don't think he'll be too happy to leap off dry ground and into a raging creek."

"Happy or not, you have to make him do it," he yelled above the roar of the rain and thunder. "Mount up and I'll throw you a rope."

Seeing no other way, Bella followed his instructions and climbed into the saddle. Noah rode closer and tossed her the end of a lariat.

"Tie that around the horn. If Casper stumbles or falls it might help keep him upright."

Nodding, she looped the rope around the saddle horn and tied it as tight as her cold, wet fingers could manage.

"It's tied. Now what?"

"Make him jump toward me. Once he gets his feet under him we'll head back in that direction." He pointed to the east and Bella nodded that she understood his instructions, but following them through was going to be another matter.

Bella didn't have time to sit there worrying or trying to gather her courage. With each passing minute the water was rising. If they didn't get out of the canyon soon they were going to be swept away completely.

Fighting the urge to close her eyes, she kicked Casper forward. When he halted at the edge, she smooched to him and gave him a tap on the rump. He leaped and as they hit the water, it splashed all around her, momentarily blinding her. Beneath her, she could feel the horse stumbling, falling to his knees. Water filled her boots and soaked her jeans all the way to her waist, but she hardly noticed the discomfort. Instead her entire focus was on lifting the reins in an effort to help the animal stay upright.

"Hang on, Bella! Don't let him fall."

Somehow the horse found stable footing and with great relief, she slumped weakly forward in the saddle, but there was hardly time to catch her breath before the tug of the lariat reminded her that they had to keep moving.

It took them more than a half hour to navigate their way back to the point from where they could climb the canyon wall and finally reach safety. There were several times Bella wondered if she could go on. Between her heart racing with fear and the struggle to ride over such rough terrain, she was exhausted.

When they finally finished the climb and arrived on top of the mesa, Noah suggested they dismount and allow the horses to rest. Bella wholly agreed, but she was trembling so badly she couldn't move. Noah had to literally pull her boots from the stirrups and lift her out of the saddle.

Once she was in his arms, they both sank to the ground where Noah tucked her head to the middle of his chest and buried his face in her wet hair.

"Oh, Lord, Bella, I thought I was going to find you drowned or dead from a lightning strike!"

Her arms barely found the strength to wrap around his neck. "Noah! When I saw you riding toward me, I—you were an answered prayer."

Clutching her tightly against him, he stroked his fingers through the soppy clumps of her hair. "I couldn't believe it when I saw you and Casper on that ledge! You crazy little fool! I told you not to ride in the canyon alone! I told you it was dangerous!"

Rearing her head back, she looked at him. "That's right. You've told me just about everything, except what I want to hear. Please, don't scold me, Noah. Not after what we've just gone through. You can do that later. Just tell me—"

He stopped her next words with a kiss that was both desperate and exhilarating. Then leaning his head back, he looked straight into her eyes. "All right, Bella. We'll go to Arizona. Together. Is that what you want to hear?"

With a cry of joy, she hugged him tightly. "It's a start."

On late Saturday evening, Bella and Noah's flight touched down at Tucson International Airport. From there they took a rental car to a downtown hotel where Bella had already reserved their rooms for the night.

While she dealt with the task of checking in, Noah waited in the lobby with their luggage. Since it was the weekend, the hotel was bustling with guests and hotel staff, but Noah hardly noticed the comings and goings around him. Beyond the wall of plate glass, a view of Tucson spread out beneath a blazing summer sun. Yet the buildings with their Spanish architecture and desert landscaping barely caught his attention. It was the wilderness beyond that grabbed his thoughts and hurled them back to the time when he had ridden over similar jagged hills and through stands of ancient saguaros, their arms lifted toward the blue heaven.

"All set," Bella suddenly spoke behind him. "We're on the seventh floor."

Pulling himself out of his memories, he turned to her and was immediately whammed all over again. A turquoise sundress hugged her slender waist while intricately designed cowboy boots covered her feet. Silver set with green malachite hung from her ears and adorned her wrist. But as always, it was the soft, tender smile on her face that made her incredibly beautiful.

Throughout the flight, he'd struggled to keep his eyes off her, but now that they were on solid ground, it was clear that keeping his hands to himself was going to be even more of a problem. More than two weeks had passed since the two of them had been intimate and the memory still continued to haunt him. For reasons he didn't want to examine, being in her arms that night had left him feeling particularly vulnerable and when she'd pushed him to talk about his past, everything about Ward and Camilla had come tumbling out of him.

He'd behaved like a jackass and stormed out, but that had been the only thing left for him to do. Except stay and admit to Bella that he'd fallen in love with her. And he'd not been ready for that. He didn't think he'd ever be ready to surrender that much of himself to anyone.

Picking up the bags, he said, "Fine with me. Let's go."

They walked to the nearest elevator and took a quick ride to the seventh floor. When they stepped off, Noah asked, "Which way to our rooms?"

"This way," she answered, pointing to their right. "But before we get there I—uh—should tell you we only have one room."

He dropped one of the bags in order to clasp his hand around her upper arm. "What do you mean, one room? I told you to book two?"

As Noah watched a soft pink color sweep across her cheeks, he knew he was in even more trouble than he thought. It was bad enough that he hadn't touched her in days, but now he was going to be sequestered in the same bedroom with her.

Her brown eyes glinted. "That would've only been a waste of money. Besides, you don't have to sleep with me unless you want to. The room is equipped with two queen-sized beds."

Unless he wanted to? Hell, for the past two weeks that's all he'd been wanting. But he'd been fighting the urge, just as he'd been fighting his feelings. Ever since he'd found her in the canyon looking half-drowned, huddling next to her horse, his emotions for the woman had been growing like a tumbleweed in a stiff wind. Yeah, he could admit that to himself, but he couldn't let Bella in on his secret. Not now or ever.

He dropped his hold on her arm and picked up the bag. "And we're damned well going to use them," he promised.

She rolled her eyes at him. "Whatever you say, Noah. I wouldn't want to make you do anything against your will."

The absurdity of her remark pulled a short laugh

from him and the sound must have shocked Bella because she stared at him in comical disbelief.

"Noah, I think that's the first time I've ever heard you laugh." Smiling happily, she looped her arm through his and urged him down the corridor. "Come on, let's go find our room and get comfortable."

Although, Bella would've preferred to order their evening meal through room service, Noah insisted they go down and eat in one of the restaurants inside the huge hotel.

She didn't argue the point. After all, just getting Noah to this point was a miracle in itself and for the past two days she'd been wondering what had finally pushed him to decide to make this trip to Arizona.

Clearly the trauma of the storm had done something to him. Even so, she still didn't know what he was actually thinking or feeling. That evening, when the two of them had finally returned to her house, Jett had been there, anxiously waiting to make sure the two of them were unharmed. With her brother there, she'd expected Noah to make a quick exit. Instead he'd hung around to care for the horses and the sopping wet saddles and blankets. Later, he'd even made coffee for the three of them and once Jett had finally departed, she'd decided Noah would stay with her. At least long enough for them to make love. Instead, he'd asked her to make travel arrangements for the two of them, then given her an abrupt goodbye. Now she was beginning to doubt he'd ever want to take her to bed again.

"Thank you for dinner, Noah. It was delicious," she told him, once they'd had their meal and returned to their room. "You know what I was thinking while we were eating?"

He loosened the bolo tie around his neck and Bella allowed her hungry gaze to travel over his tall, muscular body. Other than the day at Skylar's birthday party, she'd never seen him in anything other than jeans or cowboy gear. He looked exceptionally handsome dressed in dark, Western-cut trousers, expensive alligator boots and a tailored white shirt. Yet she had to admit that she loved seeing him best in his chinks and spurs, his dusty felt pulled down on his forehead. That was her Noah. Her rugged rancher.

"That you shouldn't have ordered green sauce on your enchiladas?"

Laughing, she sank onto a small couch near the window and began to tug off her boots. "The sauce was scorching," she admitted, "but it was delicious. No, I was thinking how this is the first time you and I have ever been anywhere together—off the J Bar S, that is."

He shot her a wry glance. "There for a while during the storm, I thought I'd be attending your funeral about now."

"You probably imagined burying Casper, too," she added thoughtfully, then shook her head. "God, if I had caused that horse to be hurt, I would've never forgiven myself."

"I'm glad to know you care that much about Casper."

A knowing smile tilted her lips. "Well, I wouldn't have wanted you to be hurt, either."

Without making a reply, he walked over to the window and for long moments Bella sat there watching him stare out at the darkening sky. Whatever was on his mind, she wanted him to share it with her. But would he ever want to share that deeper part of him, she wondered. Would this meeting with Camilla finally open his heart? Or would seeing Verde Canyon make him even more disenchanted?

Rising from the couch, she went to stand by his side. "I don't believe I've thanked you for saving my life."

"You're being melodramatic. You're a smart, strong girl. You would have eventually gotten out of the canyon on your own."

She didn't bother to argue that point, instead, she said, "I realize you don't want to be here with me. And you certainly don't want to meet with Camilla tomorrow. But I'm very glad that you are."

His blue eyes were dark with doubtful shadows as he glanced at her. "You have a misguided notion that seeing Verde Canyon is going to be cathartic for me— that suddenly I'll be liberated from all the hell Camilla and Ward put me through. Bella, nothing will ever wipe that from my mind."

She rested her hand on his arm. "You're right. Nothing ever will. But once you face this woman, I believe you can look past all the wrong. You'll be able to see the future and maybe then you can see me sharing it with you."

With a groan of misgiving, Noah turned and reached for her hands. "Where do you find this faith in me, Bella? You should've tossed in your chips long ago and told me to get lost. I'm not the sort of man a woman can understand, much less cozy up to."

Slipping her arms around his waist, she pressed her body next to his. "I find it oh, so easy to cozy up to you, Noah."

Desire stirred low in his belly, prompting him to close his eyes and push his fingers into her dark, silky hair. "Taking you to bed isn't going to fix anything," he murmured thickly.

"It will fix this ache I have to be in your arms," she whispered. "That's all I'm asking for tonight. Tomorrow— well, we can talk about promises then."

Aching. Longing. That's all he'd been doing since that Sunday afternoon so long ago when she'd shown up at his cabin.

"There might not be any promises tomorrow," he hedged.

Her arms tightened around him as her cheek came to rest against the middle of his chest. "I'm willing to take my chances."

He didn't deserve this woman. And he was fairly certain that after they met with Camilla tomorrow, Bella would realize it, too. But for tonight he wanted to hold her, love her and pretend that she would always belong to him.

Groaning with a need that was blurring his senses, he lowered his mouth to hers.

Chapter Eleven

The next morning the sun had just begun to climb above the stark, jagged mountains rimming the city, when Bella and Noah sat down at the little table in their room to eat a breakfast of chorizo omelets and warm tortillas.

Waking up next to Noah had been bittersweet for Bella. For long minutes she'd lain there listening to the even sound of his breathing and savoring the warmth of his hard body nestled close against hers. Last night she'd sensed an urgency to his lovemaking. As though it might be the last time they would be together. It was a thought Bella refused to contemplate.

Now, as she forced each bite of food down her throat, she wondered what the day was going to bring to him and to her. This morning, he looked incredibly handsome with his black hair slicked back from his rugged face and a pale blue shirt covering his broad shoul-

ders. Yet the tense lines etched around his mouth and
eyes told her he was dreading the forthcoming meeting with Camilla.

Bella was dreading it, too. From what he'd told her,
the woman had tried every way possible to seduce him.
The idea made her cringe and yet she had to believe that
this whole trip would be a turning point for Noah. Because no matter what happened with the two of them
in the future, she wanted him to be happy.

She sipped her coffee and hoped it would push the
food past her tight throat. "There's something I've been
wondering about, Noah."

With a wry grunt, he looked up from his food. "Just
something? I've been wondering about a million things.
Like what the hell am I doing here? Jett and Sassy were
going to a horse sale up at Reno today. I should've been
there to handle the barn chores. Instead, I'm nearly
a thousand miles away about to meet with a woman
who not only stabbed me in the back but also deceived
and manipulated her own husband. Even a psychiatrist
couldn't figure out what I'm doing—that's how stupid
this whole thing feels to me."

She let out a long breath. "I'll be honest, Noah. Half
the time I'm thinking exactly like you are. But then I
keep thinking about the short letter she sent you. Instead of her phone number, she gave you her lawyer's
number. What exactly did he say when you called to let
him know you'd be coming to the ranch today?"

He shrugged, but Bella knew he was feeling anything but casual. "Only that Camilla would be pleased.
And that she didn't want to talk with me over the phone.
That everything she wanted to say needed to be said
in person."

"Well, it won't be long now until we find out what's

on her mind," Bella said. "How long will it take us to drive from here to the ranch?"

"About an hour and a half. Was there anything you wanted to see or do before we leave the city this morning? I told the lawyer, if all went as planned, we'd be at the ranch by ten-thirty. We're ahead of schedule."

He glanced at the silver watch on his wrist and it dawned on Bella that this was the first time she'd seen him wearing a timepiece. Which only pointed out that he was a free-spirited cowboy who only conformed to the norm whenever he was forced to.

"Thanks for asking, but I'd rather we go on," she told him. "That way you can point out some of the landmarks along the way."

"Fine. The sooner we get this over with, the better," he said.

Two hours later, Noah slowed the car as it passed over a wide cattle guard. Above it, a wooden sign hung from a simple arch made of rough cedar post.

Verde Canyon. In Noah's wildest dreams he'd never imagined he'd be back on this desert ranch. He'd never expected to ever see the house where he and Ward had shared meals and laughter and good times. He'd been a different man then. One that he no longer recognized. Would Bella have loved that Noah? The question was moot, he realized. If not for the break between him and Ward, he and Bella would've never met. That was something he'd never thought about until now. And suddenly the ache in his chest wasn't quite as hard to bear.

"This is beautiful, Noah," Bella commented as he drove slowly over the narrow dirt road. "It's so stark and wild. The mountains are very different than the ones around the J Bar S."

He glanced over at her. "Not a damned thing on them except mesquite bosque, creosote bush and a little desert grass. But there's something pretty about them. Especially after the rain comes and it all turns green. I'm surprised you like it."

Smiling faintly, she reached for his hand and he gave it to her.

"You still think of this area as your home, don't you?"

"Doesn't make sense, does it? I went through hell here, but yes, this was my home. I'd planned to stay here for the rest of my life. Guess it's hard to get something that deep out of your head."

"And your heart," she added knowingly.

He let out a long breath. "Yeah, I used to have one of those. For your sake, Bella, I wish I could get it back."

Ten minutes later they arrived at the ranch house, a rambling one-story hacienda with a beautiful tiled roof and a ground-level porch with arched supports. Red blooming bougainvillea grew up the walls, while huge terracotta pots filled with cactus and succulents lined the edge of the porch and the walkway. One lone mesquite tree cast a flimsy shade across the east end of the small yard.

Except for the mesquite tree being a bit larger, everything looked the same as he remembered. Noah wasn't sure that was a good thing or bad. One thing was certain, though—without Ward around, the ranch wasn't the same.

"Where is the ranch yard?" Bella asked as he parked in front of a low fence made of cedar rails.

"About a quarter mile on down the road," he answered. "You can see it from the back of the house."

He looked over at her. "Ready for this?"

"I'm ready. But before we go in, Noah, I think—well, maybe it would be better if you talked with Camilla alone. Whatever she has to say to you is personal and I—"

He interrupted her words with a shake of his head. "If what she has to say can't be said in front of you, then I don't want to hear it. Okay?"

"Okay."

They walked side by side to the front door. Noah's short knock was quickly answered by a young Hispanic maid with a wide smile and black hair twisted into a ballerina bun. She ushered them through a short foyer and into a long, casually furnished living room.

"Please have a seat and make yourself comfortable," she said warmly. "I'll tell Ms. Stevens that you've arrived."

The maid disappeared through an arched doorway at the far end of the room. Noah and Bella sat down close together on a green leather couch to wait.

"This is quite a house," Bella said as she glanced up at the cathedral ceiling supported by dark wooden beams.

Strategically placed skylights sent shafts of light spreading across a floor of Spanish tile, while here and there huge pots, filled with more cactus, gave the impression that the room was an extension of the outdoors. Except for changes in the furniture, it looked the same to Noah. And everywhere his gaze landed, he was reminded of Ward. The reality of the man's death was still hard for him to absorb.

"Ward didn't hold back when he had this house built. He wanted Camilla to have the best," he added stiffly. "Poor bastard. I hope he never knew what really happened—that Camilla lied and deceived him."

"Noah, you can't mean that," Bella said in a hushed voice. "I thought you wanted your friend to know the truth."

He shook his head. "Back then, I did. Now, I realize it would have hurt him even more. And he didn't deserve that."

She rested her hand on his arm. "You didn't deserve it either, Noah."

Her brown eyes were full of empathy, but Noah could also see courage and strength radiating from her and in that moment he realized that she was all he'd ever needed or wanted. If today he lost his job, the money and cattle he'd accumulated, every possession he owned, he could survive. But losing Bella would be like losing the air he breathed. Dear God, why had it taken him so long to realize the truth?

The sound of footsteps interrupted the self-directed question and he looked around to see the maid reentering the room. Camilla Stevens followed a few steps behind her.

Like the house and the land, Ward's wife hadn't changed all that much. At thirty-eight, the woman was still slender and attractive. Her blond hair was long and coiled into a neat twist at the back of her head, while her white dress and black heels implied she was planning to go out later.

Bella's fingers suddenly tightened on his arm and he knew that no matter what transpired with this woman, she was counting on him to remain a gentleman. He couldn't let her down. Now or ever.

Barely conscious of what he was doing, Noah rose to his feet and Bella quickly joined him.

"Hello, Noah. Thank you for coming," Camilla said and reached to shake his hand.

Though it pained him, Noah complied. Mercifully, the handshake was brief and then Camilla turned her attention to Bella.

"This is Bella Sundell," Noah quickly introduced. "She made the trip with me."

The two women exchanged greetings and then Camilla gestured toward the couch. "Please sit," she said, "and Lolita will bring refreshments. Since it's still early you might prefer coffee or hot tea?"

"Coffee would be nice," Bella spoke up.

Noah merely nodded. It was hard to look at Camilla without thinking of Ward and as she took a seat in an armchair across from them, memories of his old friend rushed at him from every direction.

Camilla instructed the maid, then settled back in the chair.

Noah said, "I'm sorry about Ward. It's hard for me to believe he's gone."

"It's still hard for me to believe it, too," she said quietly, then suddenly looked away.

As Noah watched her eyes blink rapidly, he reminded himself that the woman was one of the biggest liars he'd ever met. Yet watching her now, he got the feeling that her husband's death had affected her deeply. Which didn't make sense. Seven years ago, when Noah left this ranch, she seemed to have forgotten she had a husband at all.

"I'm sorry," she said. "Ward wouldn't like me choking up like this. He wanted me to be brave."

"What happened?" Noah asked. "Your letter said his health had been declining. What was wrong?"

Camilla nodded. "For the past year and a half. He developed a lung disease—some long name I can't pronounce or even remember. In the beginning the doctors assured us it was a controllable condition. But Ward didn't respond to the treatments. We went to the best specialist, but nothing seemed to help. It was hell watching him die a little each day."

Noah let out a long breath and looked over at Bella to see she'd been touched by Camilla's recounting. Surprisingly, he'd been affected by it, too. He'd not expected Ward's wife to express any grief over his passing. The Camilla he remembered had turned cold and callous. This woman sitting in front of them acted as though she'd loved Ward deeply. It didn't make sense.

Just as an awkward silence settled over the room, Lolita returned with a tray. After the young woman had passed around cups of coffee, Camilla spoke again.

"Noah, before I get into the reason I asked you here, I want to say how sorry I am for everything that happened all those years ago. I realize that doesn't mean much. But I—well, all I can say is that I was having deep emotional problems at the time. When I lost the baby it was like I'd lost everything. I felt guilty because I couldn't give Ward the one thing he wanted. Especially after he'd given me so much. I don't know—something snapped in me. I was jealous of you, Noah. I believed Ward cared more about you than he did me."

"Camilla, that's crazy," Noah told her. "He loved you more than anything."

"Yes, it took a long time, plus a doctor's care, for me to finally realize the truth and come to my senses. But by then the harm had already been done."

Noah gripped his coffee cup as strange emotions suddenly surged inside him. This wasn't the way he'd expected Camilla to sound or behave. He'd not imagined her being apologetic or grieving.

"If you don't mind my asking," Bella spoke up, "did

you ever talk to your husband about Noah? Explain what really happened?"

Sighing heavily, Camilla placed her cup on a nearby table, then folded her hands in her lap. As Noah waited for her answer, he noticed she was still wearing her wedding rings.

"Yes. But not until recently. For years I tried to find the courage to confess the truth to him. I recognized it was wrong to let him keep thinking Noah had betrayed him. Ward had loved Noah like a son. I believed if he ever found out I'd deliberately torn them apart, he would never forgive me. But once I accepted the fact that he didn't have long to live, I couldn't hold it inside any longer. About three weeks ago, I told him the whole sordid story."

Noah and Bella exchanged pointed looks.

Noah instinctively reached for Bella's hand. "How did he react?"

Camilla dabbed a tissue beneath her eyes and though Noah would have liked to think she was shedding crocodile tears, he recognized they were real.

"Naturally he was devastated. He was ashamed of the way he'd treated you. And mercifully he forgave me. Thank God he understood that the woman I was then wasn't the same woman he'd been married to for all these years." She rose from the armchair and began to walk restlessly around the room. "After that, he hired a private investigator to locate you. He wanted to see you—to ask for your forgiveness. We'd just discovered you were working on the J Bar S and I was in the process of contacting you when Ward suddenly took a turn for the worse and died."

"Too late," Noah muttered regretfully.

Camilla paused in the middle of the room, her rue-

ful gaze passing from Noah to Bella, then back to him.
"Yes. Too late. I was a coward. I should have confessed
to him years before. Instead I lived with the lies. It
hasn't been easy."

A few weeks ago, Noah would have been consumed
with anger for this woman. The urge to jump to his feet
and choke her would've been his first instinct. But he
was feeling none of that and the realization stunned
him. Why wasn't he angry? Where were all those bitter emotions he'd been harboring for all these years? It
didn't make sense.

*Once you face this woman, I believe you can look
past all the wrong. You'll be able to see the future and
maybe then you can see me sharing it with you.*

He turned his gaze on Bella as her words whispered
through his jumbled thoughts. Oh God, how had she
known? How had she guessed that revisiting a nightmare would actually jolt him awake?

Bella's fingers tightened around his. "Noah? Are you
okay?" she asked softly.

"I'm fine. Really," he assured her and he couldn't
have meant it more. He inclined his head to Camilla,
who was now standing on the opposite side of the room,
staring sadly out the window. "I need to say some things
to her."

Smiling gently, she nodded. "I'll wait here."

Rising from the couch, Noah went to stand next to
the other woman. She looked around at him, her expression one of fatal acceptance.

"Camilla, you need to quit torturing yourself. You're
not the only one who's been a coward all these years.
I've been a bigger one. I should've found the guts to
come back to Verde Canyon and face Ward again. Instead, I thought running away was the answer. I was

wrong. We've both been wrong. I think it's time we let our mistakes go. Don't you?"

The anguish on Camilla's face slowly dissolved and a hopeful smile replaced it. "Thank you, Noah. Coming from you—well, it's the best medicine I could ever get. And now I'd like for you and Ms. Sundell to meet someone. He's waiting in the study with something to tell you."

Expecting Camilla was going to introduce them to the ranch manager, Noah collected Bella from the couch and the two of them followed her down a long tiled hallway until they reached a pair of closed wooden doors.

Noah had been in this very room many times. He and Ward had often talked over the business dealings of the ranch within these same walls. Now as the three of them stepped into the quiet space, he spotted a gray-haired man in a charcoal-colored suit sitting behind a large mahogany desk.

As soon as the elderly gentleman spotted their entrance, he politely rose to his feet.

"This is Harrison Grimes," Camilla quickly introduced. "He's been our family lawyer for several years."

With his arm wrapped tightly against the back of Bella's waist, Noah stepped forward.

"Nice to meet you, Mr. Grimes," Noah said, then gestured to Bella. "This is Bella Sundell. She's also a family lawyer."

"Oh!" Camilla exclaimed, then studied the both of them with confusion. "I thought she—Ms. Sundell came as your—friend. Did you think you were going to need a lawyer?"

Noah shook his head, then cast Bella a pointed look. "No. Bella is here because I—wanted her to be with me. Because we—we're together."

Camilla smiled with relief. "That's good," she said, then turned her attention to the lawyer. "So why don't you explain to them what's going on, Harrison."

"Certainly," he said, then tapped a legal document lying on the center of the desk. "Camilla has asked me to be here this morning so that I can answer any questions you might have concerning Ward's will."

"Will. What does Ward's will have to do with me?" Noah questioned.

The lawyer arched an inquisitive brow at Camilla. "You haven't told him yet?"

The woman shook her head. "No. I thought you could do a better job of it."

Harrison Grimes pointed to a pair of wing-back chairs sitting at an angle to the desk. "Perhaps you two better sit down."

"Yes," Camilla quickly added. "I'm sorry. With everything going on, I've forgotten my manners. Please sit."

Once Bella and Noah had made themselves comfortable, the lawyer eased down into the desk chair, then leveled a benevolent look on Noah.

"No matter how I say it, this is probably going to come as quite a shock," the lawyer said. "So I won't beat around the bush. You see, before Ward died, he instructed me to change his will in order to make sure that Verde Canyon and all of its holdings would go to you."

Noah was so stunned he was certain the breath had been knocked out of him. Shaking his head, he squinted at the lawyer. "Me? You're saying the Verde is mine?"

"That's right. The land, the house and other buildings, along with all the cattle and horses. Basically everything is yours now." He picked up the legal document and handed it to Bella. "Since you're a lawyer, Ms. Sundell, you might want to look through this. I'm sure you can explain anything Mr. Crawford doesn't understand."

Completely dazed, Noah shook his head once again. "I don't need legal explanations. I just—why did Ward do this? The illness must have affected his sanity!"

"I assure you that Ward had all his mental faculties before he died. This was his last wish. That you become the sole owner of Verde Canyon Ranch."

Bella appeared to be just as stunned as Noah and she looked inquiringly at Camilla. "What about you, Mrs. Stevens? Surely you can't be happy about this?"

Camilla merely smiled. "I couldn't be happier. If our child had lived, the ranch certainly would have gone to him or her. As it is, Noah is the closest thing Ward had to a son. He truly wanted to make up for the past. Plus, he died with the assurance that the ranch would remain in capable hands."

"And if you're thinking that Camilla has been left out in the cold, don't," the lawyer interjected. "Over the years Ward made some excellent investments. Camilla is getting more than enough to make sure her future is financially secure."

"But this is your home, Camilla," Noah pointed out. "What—"

"Don't worry," she said with a wry little laugh. "I'll be moving out next week. I'm going to live near my parents down in southern California."

She glanced at the dainty gold watch on her wrist. "Now if you two won't mind, I need to be going or I'll be late for church services. Please make yourself at home and look around all you want. I'm sure there's plenty you'll want to look over and talk about. If you need anything, Harrison will be here, as well as Lolita."

* * *

A few minutes later, after Camilla had departed, Bella and Noah walked across the backyard until they reached the split-rail fence. From where they stood in the hot sun, they could see the working ranch yard in the distance. Dust was boiling up from a network of cattle pens and the faint yips and yells from a group of cowboys could be heard on the desert wind. Nearby, the hills were covered with patches of cacti, creosote and blooming yucca.

Bella took in the beautiful sight and tried to imagine what Noah was thinking and feeling at this moment. He'd just become a rich man and she could only wonder what this might do to their fragile relationship.

"I thought coming down here and meeting with Camilla would be good for you," Bella said thoughtfully. "But I never imagined anything like this was going to happen."

He lifted his hat from his head and raked a hand through the black waves. "It's still hard for me to take in, Bella. I thought Ward hated me. To think he's given me everything he worked for—I feel pretty damned humble right now. Not to mention feeling like a bastard," he tacked on, his voice gruff.

She frowned at him. "I don't understand."

He tugged the hat back onto his head. "All these years I've been simmering with resentment. Like a bulldog I hung on to the fact that I'd been wronged. I should've forgiven Camilla and Ward a long time ago." His arm slipped around her shoulders and drew her to his side. "That chip you talked about on my shoulder— I wore it like a badge. I've been such a fool!"

"All of that is over now," she said gently. "Truly over."

He made a sweeping gesture with his arm. "What am I going to do with all of this, Bella?"

She glanced up at him, her heart pounding with uncertainty. "You're going to keep it, of course. Verde Canyon is your ranch now—the place you call home."

With his hands on her shoulders, he pulled her around so that she was facing him.

"Home is where you are, Bella. It's taken me a long time to realize that. And as much as I love Verde Canyon, I love you even more. I want you to be my wife. But I can't ask you to make your home here with me."

I love you even more.

His words poured into her heart, healing every ache, and pushing out the last vestige of loneliness.

Resting her palms against his chest, she tilted her head back to meet his gaze. "Why can't you ask me?"

His eyes widened. "Why? Because it wouldn't be right. You have your own beautiful home on the J Bar S."

"And it's empty without you in it."

"You have your law practice in Carson City."

"I can practice law anywhere," she reasoned.

His head swung back and forth as though he couldn't believe what he was hearing. "You're very close to your brother and his family. You wouldn't want to live far away from them."

"Jett and Sassy are building their own lives together," she pointed out. "It's time I quit being just a sister and an aunt. I want to be a wife and a mother. Besides, whenever we get the urge to see them, we can always fly up for visits."

His arms formed a tight circle around her. "You make it all sound so easy."

"Loving you is very easy, my darling."

Bending his head, he brought his lips next to hers.

"Today I've become a very rich man, Bella. Not because I inherited the Verde, but because I have you and your love. I hope you'll always remember that."

Happiness glowed in her eyes as she smiled up at him. "Don't worry. I'll never let you forget it."

Chuckling, he covered her mouth with a long, tender kiss that melted her bones even more than the hot Arizona sun.

When he finally lifted his head, she grabbed his hand and urged him toward an opening in the fence. "Come on, I want you to show me around the ranch. I need to pick out a perfect spot to pasture Mary Mae and Casper. Are there any canyons around here I can ride down?"

Laughing now, Noah slipped his arm around the back of her waist and urged her toward the ranch yard. "A few. But from now on I'll be riding right beside you."

Her heart brimming with happiness, she laughed along with him. "I'm going to hold you to that promise."

Epilogue

Six months later, on a cool November afternoon, Bella had just gotten home from a short shopping trip and was putting away the last of her grocery purchases when Noah entered the kitchen and announced he had a surprise to show her.

Now, as he led her into a big barn where most of the hay for Verde Canyon was stored, she looked curiously around the cavernous interior. "Noah, if you've bought me a piece of jewelry and hidden it somewhere in all this hay, you're going to have to dig it out," she warned teasingly. "And I could've told you I'd rather have a pair of cowboy boots than a diamond."

He laughed, something he did quite often these days. Bella had come to love the sound just as much as she loved her new home in the Arizona desert. With ranch hands that liked and respected him and a cow/calf operation that continued to produce, she could safely say that Noah was happily living out his dream of managing Verde Canyon.

After that memorable day they'd learned Noah had inherited the Verde, they'd flown back to Nevada. A few days later, they'd been married in the same small church Bella and Jett had attended since their childhood. Sassy had helped her find a beautiful dress in champagne-colored lace and Peta had taken over the task of decorating the church with candles and flowers. With only family and a few close friends in attendance it had been a simple, yet beautiful ceremony.

Jett and Sassy had been totally shocked by the news of Ward's will. Although they were extremely happy for both Noah and Bella, it was obvious Jett hated to see his new brother-in-law leave his position on the J Bar S. And he was especially emotional to see his sister move away.

Not about to leave Jett shorthanded, Noah had hung on as foreman for three more weeks in order to give Jett time to find a man to replace him. Bella had used that length of time to pack her belongings for shipping and close all her cases at the law office. As for her house, she'd turned it over to Jett to use however he chose.

With so much to do regarding the move to Arizona, Bella and Noah had forgone a honeymoon. But their lives had quickly settled into a comfortable groove and since then Noah kept offering to take Bella on a short trip to some exotic island. But as far as she was concerned, spending each day with her husband was a honeymoon for her.

As for Bella practicing law, a couple of months ago, she'd opened a little office in Tombstone in a building that had originally been used for a saloon. So far her work was sporadic, but it kept her busy for three days a week and that was more than enough to keep her content.

"Christmas is only a month away. If you're good, Santa might bring you a new pair of boots."

Noah's reminder pulled her away from her pleasant thoughts and she shot him an impish grin. "Hmm. If that's the case, these next few weeks I'll try to be on my best behavior."

"Yeah, I know what you consider good behavior," he said with a hungry growl, then pulled her into his arms and kissed her. "Like taking me to bed in the middle of the day."

Her lips tilted provocatively against his. "A cowboy needs a little rest now and then."

He kissed her one more time, then took her by the hand and led her over to a deep crevice in the hay.

"Take a look in there."

Bella did as he instructed and immediately let out a delighted yelp. A gray momma cat was curled around three little yellow fur balls. "Baby kittens! How precious! When did this happen?"

"Yesterday afternoon, I saw mother cat still looking like she'd swallowed a watermelon crossing the ranch yard, heading this way. But I didn't hear the faint meows until this morning."

Tapping a thoughtful finger against her chin, she asked sagely, "So do I need to ask who the father is?"

Chuckling, Noah pointed to the top of the haystack where a big yellow tom sat preening his fur.

"Jack!" Bella called up to the cat. "You naughty guy!"

"Yep, Jack has a family now," Noah said. "I think

we can safely say he's made himself a permanent home on the Verde."

She gave her husband a shrewd smile. "I hope you look as proud as Jack does whenever our baby is born."

An odd look came over his features, then suddenly a wondrous light filled his eyes. "Bella—are you—does this mean what I'm thinking?"

Her heart overflowing with love, she stepped into the circle of his arms. "It means we're going to have a baby. The doctor is predicting it will arrive sometime in mid-May."

"Doctor? You've already been to see a doctor?" he asked, excitement filling his voice.

"I saw him this morning—that's why I drove in to Tucson."

"And you told me you were going grocery shopping for Thanksgiving dinner!" He scolded. "Sneaky! Sneaky!"

Her grin was completely guilty. "I wanted to surprise you. I did go grocery shopping. After I made a stop at the health clinic." Her hands reached up and cradled his face. "Are you happy?"

"I've got a bigger smile than Jack does right now. Why wouldn't I be happy?"

She traced her fingertips along his cheekbone and marveled at how much their love had filled their lives with happiness and meaning.

"There was a time when you said you didn't want to be a husband or father," she gently reminded him.

"I never thought I had the qualifications to be a dad. And I sure didn't want to make a mess of things, the way my old man had with me. But that was before I knew someone believed in me. Like you."

"And Ward," she added softly. "Wherever he is now, he's smiling because you're happy."

"I think so, too," he agreed. "And coming from me, this might sound crazy, but I'm actually glad things are working out for Camilla."

He'd learned the blessings of forgiveness and Bella couldn't be happier about the change it had made in him. "From the short letter she sent us, it sounds like she's making a fresh start to her life. I certainly wish her well." Pressing herself closer to his rugged body, she splayed her hands against his back. "And now that we're talking about fresh starts, I've been thinking it's time I made a search for your mother."

He looked stunned. "My mother? Why would you even be thinking of her?"

"Hmm. We're going to have a baby. The holidays are growing near and my mother is coming down for a visit, along with Jett and his family. It would be nice if you had someone in your family to share in our happiness."

"I've not seen my mother since I was a boy, Bella. I doubt you can find her."

"Does that mean you won't mind if I try?" she asked hopefully.

The radiance in his blue eyes warmed every corner of her heart.

"No. I won't mind," he said. "After all, I never could deny you anything, my sweet Bella."

"Not even a hamburger," she added slyly.

"Yeah, and look where that's gotten me," he joked, then his expression suddenly turned thoughtful as his hand rested on the lower part of her flat belly. "The middle of May, huh? The wildflowers will be gone by then. But the canyon will still be green. It'll be a beautiful time for our baby to come."

Verde Canyon. Yes, she thought, her heart overflowing with joy. They'd ride through the canyon together. Always.

* * * * *

Find the next installment of Stella Bagwell's
MEN OF THE WEST *series,*
HIS BADGE, HER BABY... THEIR FAMILY?,
coming in August 2016.